Droids to Magic

Fantastic Tales
of
Science Fiction and Wonder

Tom Marcoux

Author of *TimePulse: Beyond Titanic*

Speaker-Author of 31 books

Blogger, BeHeardandBeTrusted.com

YourBodySoulandProsperity.com

A QuickBreakthrough Publishing Edition

QuickBreakthrough Publishing is an imprint of Tom Marcoux Media, LLC. More copies are available from the publisher, Tom Marcoux Media, LLC. Please call (415) 572-6609 or write TomSuperCoach@gmail.com

or visit www.TomSuperCoach.com

or Tom's blog: www.BeHeardandBeTrusted.com

This book was developed and written with care. Names and details were modified to respect privacy.

Disclaimer: This book includes stories of fiction. Names, characters, places, and incidents are products of the author's imagination or are used fictionally. Any resemblance to actual events or locals or persons living or dead, is entirely coincidental. The author and publisher acknowledge that each person's situation is unique, and that readers have full responsibility to seek consultations with health, financial, spiritual and legal professionals. The author and publisher make no representations or warranties of any kind, and the author and publisher shall not be liable for any special, consequential or exemplary damages resulting, in whole or in part, from the reader's use of, or reliance upon, this material.

Other Books by Tom Marcoux:

- TimePulse: Beyond Titanic
- Be Heard and Be Trusted: How to Get What You Want
- Nothing Can Stop You This Year!
- Darkest Secrets of Persuasion and Seduction Masters
- Darkest Secrets of Charisma
- Darkest Secrets of Negotiation Masters
- Darkest Secrets of the Film and Television Industry Every Actor Should Know
- Darkest Secrets of Making a Pitch to the Film and Television Industry
- Darkest Secrets of Film Directing

Praise for *Droids to Magic: Fantastic Tales of Science Fiction and Wonder*

• "I really enjoyed the stories *Android Blue* and *Denise's Pieces*. This collection is a fun mix that will tease your sci-fi sweet tooth and quench your thirst for suspense." – Thomas Price, Reputation and Social Media Manager

• "*Jenalee Storm's* spunky attitude draws me in and I love reading about the power she discovers...and...*Jack AngelSword* fights to save the most precious person in his life—and it's a compelling read to see what he will do for that 6-year-old." – Lisa Lumos, Graphic Novel Artist, Illustrator, Caricaturist

Praise for Tom Marcoux's Other Work:

• "*TimePulse: Beyond Titanic* is an action-filled Sci-Fi adventure. Its fast-paced tone makes it a summer popcorn movie in a book." – Danek S. Kaus, Produced Screenwriter and author of *Swords of the Dead*.

• "In *Reduce Clutter, Enlarge Your Life*, Marcoux will help you get rid of the physical and mental clutter occupying precious space in your life. You'll reclaim wasted energy, lower your stress, and find time for new opportunities." – Laura Stack, author of *Execution IS the Strategy*

• "In *Reduce Clutter, Enlarge Your Life*, Marcoux will help you get rid of the physical and mental clutter occupying precious space in your life. You'll reclaim wasted energy, lower your stress, and find time for new opportunities." – Laura Stack, author of *Execution IS the Strategy*

• "*Create Your Best Life* helps you learn skills in persuasion, charisma, confidence, influence and emotional strength. This is *the book* that helps you get great things done!" – Dr. JoAnn Dahlkoetter, author of *Your Performing Edge* and coach to CEOs and Olympic Gold Medalists

• "In *Darkest Secrets of Persuasion and Seduction Masters*, learn useful countermeasures to protect you from being darkly manipulated." – David Barron, co-author, *Power Persuasion*

• "In *Be Heard and Be Trusted*, Tom's advice on how to remain true to yourself and establish authentic rapport with clients is both insightful and reality based. He [shows how] to establish oneself as a credible expert." -Arthur P. Ciaramicoli, Ed.D., Ph.D., author *The Curse of the Capable*

• "*Nothing Can Stop You This Year* is a treasure trove of tips, tools, and terrific ideas—practical, reassuring, and energizing! Tom provides wonderful resources for achieving your goals." – Elayne Savage, Ph.D., author of *Don't Take It Personally! The Art of Dealing with Rejection*

Visit Tom's blog: www.BeHeardandBeTrusted.com

CONTENTS

DEDICATION AND ACKNOWLEDGEMENTS

This book includes stories of fiction. Names, characters, places, and incidents are products of the author's imagination or are used fictionally. Any resemblance to actual events or locals or persons living or dead, is entirely coincidental.

This book is dedicated to the terrific film/book consultant and author Johanna Ellen Mac Leod. Johanna, thanks for your insights. Thank you to Anisa Heins for the front cover illustration. It is also dedicated to the rest of the team who helped bring these stories to fruition. Thank you for comments to Jonathan Colton, Dave Strand, Dave Thude, Thomas Price, David MacDowall Blue, Keith Grassmick, Lisa Lumos, and Kayelynn Kennedy. The stories were edited by Barry Adamson II—thanks, Barry. Thank you to David MacDowall Blue for your editing of sections of "Secrets for Your Own Creative Projects." Thank you to my parents Al Marcoux and Sumiyo Marcoux for their kindness and generosity. Thanks to Higher Power. And thanks to my clients, readers, college/graduate students and enthusiastic audiences. Thank you to the team at Tom Marcoux Media, LLC. The best to you.

Merlin's Starship

"Ensign, take over the science station," Captain Serehn said. She was formal, but had a hint of a smile.

Ensign Arthur Penn knew that the Captain had accelerated his training. He wasn't sure why, but he would do his best to live up to her expectations.

Arthur took a glance at the viewscreen. They had just entered the Tarbien nebula. Enemy ships might be in the area. All crew members were on edge.

Starting to turn his chair to glance at his small screen of the science station, Arthur saw Captain Serehn shift in her command chair.

"First Officer Potter, what is—" Captain Serehn froze in place, mid-sentence.

Arthur glanced about and saw that the First Officer and four other crew members also didn't move at all.

Still, Arthur could move easily.

From a glowing cylinder of light just five feet from Arthur, a man with a beard and in robes stepped forth.

"It's good to see you again, Arthur."

"What? I don't know you, sir," Arthur said.

"Not in this time. Not in this incarnation," the man said.

"Listen well. We have little time. I cannot hold this freeze on time much longer."

Arthur glanced at his Captain, First Officer Potter and four crew people on the bridge. Still all frozen.

"I have seen this timeline play out. This bridge will be attacked. You must take command," the man said.

"What? And who are you?"

"Merlin."

"The ancient legend?" Arthur asked.

"No time for a history lesson. You must take command. Subdue the attacker. And get this ship out of this sector," Merlin said. He gestured to those on the bridge, "Or all on this bridge and on this vessel will die."

"I'm not ready to take command. I'm just an Ensign," Arthur protested.

"Leadership means you are ready to not be ready. You decide. Moment to moment. You follow your intuition. Whatever happens, you adapt," Merlin said.

"Still, I don't have the experience to—" Arthur said.

The bridge was bathed in flickering light.

"Our time is short," Merlin said, placing a kind hand on Arthur's shoulder.

Merlin continued, "This is your time, Arthur. You have returned."

With a wave of his staff, Merlin unfroze time—and he disappeared.

The door to the bridge opened with a whoosh. Two laser-blasts burst forth. Captain Serehn and First Officer Potter took direct hits before Arthur managed to kick the weapon from the attacker's hand. In the same instant that the weapon hit a wall, Arthur kneed the attacker in the groin and elbowed him in the temple. The traitor fell, unconscious. Arthur's stomach turned: It was his friend Jerry, a fellow ensign.

Upon retrieving the weapon, Arthur tossed the weapon to Ensign Sandra Donnell.

"Watch him, Ensign. We'll interrogate him later."

From the corner of his eye, Arthur saw the viewscreen, revealing two TrinKen, enemy ships de-cloak.

Arthur said firmly, "Helix-shields up. Helm, vector 47, engage."

He turned and said, "Mr. Ventra, drop zenchu countermeasures."

Arthur watched as the crew responded at speed.

He was clear: Save the ship. Sort the regulations later.

Watching from another dimension, Merlin smiled.

Afterward to *Merlin's Starship*

"Merlin's Starship," is a science fiction adaptation regarding the Legend of King Arthur. This Legend has been an interest of mine for some time. Years ago, I wrote a science fiction screenplay *TimePulse* which focused on a young man who dedicates himself to training women in martial arts so they can protect themselves. His efforts tie into his devotion to chivalry and the positive values of King Arthur and his knights.

I published three stories in the *TimePulse* universe in my previous collection of short fiction, *Time Pulse: Beyond Titanic*—available on Amazon.com.

Android Blue

"When you going to tell him?" Mom asked.

"Never," Dad said.

"Tell me what?" I asked, entering the family living room—wearing my fresh, new police uniform for my first day of work—as a newly minted rookie cop.

"Oh—look at you! Your first day!" Mom said, a big smile on her face.

Dad put his hand on my shoulder. I could feel my father's pride in me.

"Sam, I'll drive you in," Dad suggested.

"No. I'll take the old Honda," I replied.

"You be careful, honey. Don't take any unnecessary risks," Mom said.

About fifteen minutes later, still in the Honda half-way to the precinct, I stopped at a red light outside an old warehouse.

Then I heard a scream. From inside the warehouse.

I jumped out of my car, grabbed the receiver connected to my lapel and tried to call in to ask for backup. My police radio blared static.

Hearing another scream, I drew my firearm and went in. In the dim light coming through a couple of high up windows, I saw It. Big as a horse. Tentacles. Gaping mouth. Nearby some kind of small spacecraft.

I saw the girl. 20s. Brunette, pretty. Terror on her face. She screamed. The Creature silenced the girl by biting her head off.

I fired.

A tentacle whipped out, grabbed my wrist. Some form of acid took off my hand and destroyed the gun. Pain. Searing. Horrible. Then the pain stopped instantly.

I stared at where my hand used to be. My stump had . . . circuits. What? Robot arm? I'm not all human? But—

A slimy tentacle snapped at me. I rolled out of the way.

Got to stay alive.

I tried to evade the Creature and find some kind of weapon in the warehouse. I found a pole. A seven foot long piece of steel rebar. Using my left hand and balancing with what remained of my right forearm, I used the rebar like a spear and slammed it through the Creature's grotesque head.

In its death throes the Creature shoved the rebar back, and it went through my abdomen.

The pain like fire. Some sparks burst from my abdomen. I started to feel weak.

I somehow managed to pull myself off the rebar and left it with the dead creature.

I felt pain from the surface area of my wound.

With my one hand, I fumbled with my cell phone.

Protocol. Call the station. Tell them "officer down."

No. If I survive this, I don't want them to know I'm— What am I?!

Pressed the auto dial.

No reception.

I barely made it outside, and I ducked into my car.

I drove two blocks and pulled to the side of the street. I pressed auto dial on my cell phone again.

Mom answered.

"What am I?!," I said.

"Are you all right?" she asked.

"I am . . . injured. I'm in trouble. Warehouse at 2239 Shavlin Drive. I'm in the Honda. Can't move."

It was hard to talk.

"I love you, Mom. You tell Dad, right?" I love. I know I love them so I'm not just a machine. Was I a hybrid?

"You stay on the phone, Sam," she said.

Then she called out, "Kevin! Get the emergency case. I got the address." She said to me, "You hold on, Sammy. We're on the way."

"Sammy"—Mom hadn't said that in a while.

I had protested about that name when I was a teenager.

I wanted the grown up "Sam" to be my name.

How did I grow up? When did I get this body? What am I? Do I have a . . . have a . . . soul?

Hard to think. I hold onto one idea because . . . everything else is crazy: *I love. I know I love them so I'm not just a machine.*

Mom, Dad . . . get here soon.

I want to live.

Afterward to *Android Blue*

This story began as a script for a short film and I'm now

considering expanding it into graphic novel. The purpose of this story is to explore how we choose what we value and how that defines our identity. From identity, we shape our destiny.

Denise's Pieces

My mother's severed hand fell to the floor. I did it. I had not touched her, but my mind had done it.

Seventeen years of her cutting me to the bone with her constant slicing of my self-esteem, and something snapped.

Oh, God! Oh, God! What do I do?!

She's bleeding! I moved quickly. I grabbed a dish towel and made a tourniquet to stop the bleeding from her stump.

Now what?!

Keep the hand cool!

I tossed her hand into the refrigerator. I dialed 911 on my cell phone. The operator asked me to repeat myself. I was so upset that I ran my words together.

I don't want my mom hurt. Did I put her hand in the refrigerator? Oh, yeah, I did. The hand might be preserved so surgeons could put her hand back.

Only when I was in the ambulance and the EMT was caring for my mother, did I calm down a bit. Only then did I wonder: What would be my story to the police?

No way could I say that she had grabbed me viciously

with that hand, and then, some moments later, it came off.

I looked at my shirt. A miracle. No blood on me.

I could say I found her bleeding.

* * *

The police went with the story that someone had come into the house through the backdoor. I was the scared 17 year old girl whose mother had gone through a big trauma. The one thing that impressed the police was my quick thinking.

I told them I had seen some movies and TV shows in which people did some emergency procedures. The tourniquet idea came from the film *Second Chance* and the keep the body part cool idea came from a Discovery Channel show about people surviving extreme trauma.

It seemed that the police believed me. So I was safe. Sort of.

But I knew it. I could go into a rage again and hurt somebody.

How did I know?

At the hospital, some gangbanger hit me with his shoulder. Not walking past me. Trying to walk *through* me.

Suddenly, a deep gash on his palm opened up. A cut that spontaneously appeared. A cut I knew that my mind had put there.

I got away fast, hoping that anyone would think that he'd just been in some fight.

I felt like throwing up. How could I be hurting these people?

Was I just fooling myself?

Was I holding grudges in my subconscious mind?

What the hell was going on? I had to get away from

people.

I ran out of the hospital. I saw a corner between buildings where I could duck down and hide behind a dumpster.

I sat there for—I don't know—a half an hour?

My cell phone rang. By reflex I hit the Talk button.

"I got to see your mother, and you must babysit for your niece," my Aunt Susie ordered.

"But—

"Don't tell me but! Grow up! You help your family!" My Aunt Susie hung up.

My niece, Jodie, was a brat. Maybe not all the time. Most of the time.

Sometimes, she would just piss me off. I'd watch her push a ceramic doll to the edge of a table, just watching for the horrified look on my face. Brat.

As I walked up to the door of my Aunt Susie's house, I thought, "Jodie, please, please, please don't be a brat, today!"

I stepped in, and my Aunt Susie nearly ran me over.

"Okay, Denise. You got this," Aunt Susie said over her shoulder.

"Jodie, be a good girl," Aunt Susie continued, opening the door.

"Yes, Momma," six year old Jodie said, all innocent and sugar and spice.

Barf.

Aunt Susie bought it and closed the door behind her.

Jodie took one look at me and ran over to a flower pot.

The little kid stared me down and pushed over the flower pot. CRASH.

"Damn! That little shit—"

I ran to the bathroom, slammed the door shut and locked it.

I told myself, "No, it's okay. Just a flower pot. Five bucks? I'll pay for it."

CRASH!

That doesn't matter—whatever it was. Hey, they'll never pick me to babysit ever again.

I don't want my niece to bleed!

It would serve her right.

No! This is not me. Not me!

Then I heard:

"Jodie, what are you doing?" Aunt Susie called out. "Where's Denise?"

"Bathroom," Jodie said, some triumph in her voice. Yeah, she had driven me out of the living room.

"Denise, you all right?" my Aunt Susie asked, from the other side of the bathroom door.

No, I'm not all right.

"I feel sick!" I called out.

"Jodie, did you cut your hand?" Aunt Susie asked her daughter.

Did I do that?! I wondered.

Then I glanced at the window. Slid it open and climbed out.

I ran.

Soon I was hiding in a corner of a nearby park. I curled up behind some bushes desperate no one would find me.

I didn't want to hurt anybody.

I just wanted to . . . survive.

I needed some answers. What's wrong with me?

Desperate, I searched the 'net, using my smartphone.

I used words like "Evidence mind over matter" and "Control psychic abilities."

No! My problem was anger. I can't get angry. Not now. Not ever.

"Control anger"

An Anger Management workshop was the next day.

I looked at the description with words like:

"Beneath anger is fear."

Really.

"You'll learn to use breathing techniques to calm down instantly."

Okay.

I was desperate.

I snuck back into my home. My mother was evidently still in the hospital.

How was I going to face her?

I got up early the next morning and arrived 15 minutes before the Anger Management class.

I sat in front.

I wasn't going to miss a word.

Maybe I could somehow quiet down the tornado inside.

I hope so.

Afterward to *Denise's Pieces*

I've seen that many of my best moments arose when I paused and *responded* to a dangerous situation instead of reacted. This is due to the discipline I learned in meditation before each session of karate school. Such training helped me do well in many difficult situations—including a strained relationship with my father.

Living

Chapter One

The Intruder hunted me. I looked over my shoulder and saw the Golden Gate Bridge glowing sunset red. I slipped, tipping from the cliff of the Marina Headlands. Icy waters of the San Francisco Bay raged one hundred feet below. But I caught myself. Soon, I strode near the twisted frame of a metallic banister with a white rose at its base. My Swiss army knife clanked accidentally up against it. Damn! That will reveal my location to the relentless Intruder! Behind me a large shadow raced across the ground. A huge claw scraped across the banister, generating a piercing sound that ran me through with terror.

I must face this, I thought.

I turned around and stood tall. I held my Swiss army knife down—and the knife's blade elongated, transforming into a katana. I swung the fully-formed sword up and—

The sword and the huge claw collided with sparks. Knocked to the side, I saw my reflection in a puddle left by the last rain. I saw the Intruder's reflection. There we were: man and beast locked in mortal combat. The Intruder, nine feet tall, towered over me. I struck with the sword but was hit, and I fell to the ground, my legs drenched by the puddle, with a white rose nearby. I got up, but The Intruder's next blow hurt terribly. I felt blood spurt from my mouth. Blood splattered on the white rose, spotting it with red. I stood up and struck again. My sword and the Intruder's claw ignited sparks with each blow.

A flash of light blinded me, and I suddenly fell. Horrible pain. I had two burning stumps, as my legs were cut off—mid-thigh. Perspiration stung my eyes. I looked up and saw the Intruder, towering over me. I had no way to escape—

Another flash of light—

—faded as I opened my eyes; I awakened with a start. *That's how I had escaped, by waking up.* My mouth tasting like paste, I was back to the reality of an overcast afternoon and sitting on the floor in my day camp classroom. It was a break between classes. I could see my own face reflected on the surface of my award that read: "David Nouveau, Best Day Camp Counselor of the Year." I was in my 30's, Asian eyes, European nose. My Swiss army knife was open near me, near my art project—which was similar to a paper airplane. It was actually a paper–hang-glider complete with a little paper-man.

I closed my Swiss army knife and placed it into my pocket. Then, I adjusted the Paper Hang-glider and threw it. The Paper Hang-glider flowed in the air and landed near my favorite sculpture in the whole world—a crystal figurine of a flying horse, which I called Crystal Pegasus. I had written a story about Crystal Pegasus that I told to each new session of day camp kids I encountered. For the last few years, it became my day camp kids' favorite story. And I was going to tell the new kids within the next day or two—time permitting. The suns rays flowed through the Crystal Pegasus figurine, making it glow, and near it rested my flute in its vinyl quiver. Reverently, I picked up the flute and played a tune I had written called "The Crystal Pegasus Theme." As I flowed with the music, I felt like a smiling little boy in front of a birthday cake. A clock chimed, and I looked at it. I spun my flute and smoothly slipped it into its vinyl quiver—something that I usually wore on my shoulder.

I heard little feet coming in the door. My day camp kids ran past one wall with a poster that read: "Dream-makers Day Camp." I turned on some fast beat, uplifting music. I put on sunglasses. A little boy and girl followed my lead and put on sunglasses. A minute later, I danced energetically, followed by my little day camp kids, all wearing sunglasses. It was fun, cute and uplifting. My good friend and fellow counselor, Jennifer, joined our "conga line." Her smile for me still showed gratitude that I had taken her place this morning for "meet and greet." I preferred coming in at a sane 10 AM. But Jennifer was supposed to be in at 6:30 for the kids whose power-lunch parents wanted an early start on the workday. Jennifer knew mornings were tough on me. But I said I'd cover for her. And she knew she could count on me to come through despite that I wasn't sleeping much lately. I was tired. But in the conga line I felt alive! I led them all in enjoying the moment.

That same afternoon, I sat on a bench, waiting at a bus stop. I looked up and saw an African-American elderly woman in a wheelchair moving in the crosswalk of the street. Sometime later I learned that her name was Trudy, but at this moment, she used her hands on her wheels to slowly creep forward. A passerby rushed past her, ignoring the painful progress it took her to merely cross the street. Compassion filled my heart for Trudy's plight. Then, a screeching sound—and my eyes shot towards it. The sound came from a weaving car about a block away—the car was racing toward Trudy. I had seconds to act. I jumped up, ran over to Trudy, and pushed her out of the way just as the car was going past. The car hit my back foot. Pain! Like fire. My shoe was torn from my foot and flew across the street into some bushes.

Once we were on the sidewalk, Trudy looked up from her wheelchair and asked me, "Are you all right?"

"Yeah," I said, gritting my teeth with the pain. I looked down and pulled up the bottom of my pants and saw blood oozing on my leg.

"Thank you. That was—oh, your shoe," Trudy said, noticing my shoeless foot. Her old eyes missed the blood because I had already hidden the injury on my shin. No sense in having her feel bad.

I gently placed a hand on Trudy's shoulder, gave it a reassuring squeeze. She smiled and her face glowed. Then, I walked, with a bit of a limp, toward the bush where my shoe was.

"Be good to yourself," she called after me.

At the bush, I gingerly put on my shoe, and as I stood up, I saw something visible on the other side of the bush. It was a cemetery. Near a tombstone, a man in his 30's knelt, putting flowers in a holder. He had red hair and a tightly cut beard. I saw him get up. A young woman walked up to him and slapped his face. I flinched in empathy. She rushed past the man, threw his flowers away, and placed her own flowers at the tombstone. The young man just stood there. Why would he just take that slap? I watched as he simply put on sunglasses and walked away.

About one hour later, I walked out of my doctor's building. I took a deep breath, trying to regain my composure. I saw the red-haired, young man walk past me. He went into a bar. I followed.

Within minutes I watched as the young man downed a shot of Tequila—one after another, after another. He had told me his name was Mark. The bartender walked by and Mark waved for another shot. The bartender, middle-aged, with kind eyes, looked at me significantly. I nodded that I would take care of Mark, and the bartender poured another shot.

"Anything for you?" the bartender asked.

"Another orange juice—thanks," I said.

He nodded and got me an orange juice.

Mark spoke; his voice carrying the number of drinks he already thrown back. "It just never stops. You know? You know?"

"Yeah. I—I'm with you on that. . ." I said.

"Never stops hurting. It becomes part of you. Just carry it around. Like you're dying inside."

I nodded in agreement. I knew what carrying something painful felt like.

About two hours later, I was in my apartment drinking a glass of water. Then, I played a few notes on an electronic piano, and wrote the notes on a blank sheet of music paper. My pencil tip broke. While I looked for a sharpener, my pencil rolled off my desk into an old box. I dug in the box for the pencil and accidentally discovered a photo of Carolyn, my ex-wife. Emotional pain pierced my chest. Her face.

Beautiful. The love of my life. At least then. Six years ago, our marriage had fallen to pieces. It still felt like shards of glass grinding inside my chest.

Trying to escape into music, I turned on my radio and heard an R&B song, "I Get Over You"

The music and lyrics sent me into a memory. I remembered Smoking Joe, the lead singer of our band "Smooth Ride." Smoking Joe traded lyrics with the backup singers.

"I guess I'll just get over. Get over you. I get over," Smoking Joe sang.

"Get over," backup singers answered.

"Get over you," Smoking Joe sang.

And I remembered singing backup and playing the keyboards for the band. Near the stage, Carolyn swayed with the music. Her eyes sparkled with love for me that day. She was so graceful. What a vision she was.

Still at my desk, I was lost in the memory—then the music faded, and I snapped out of it. I couldn't take any other music at that point, and I turned off the radio. I happened to look downward and saw, in the box, a newspaper clipping that read: "Fans Ask: What Happened to David Nouveau?" I felt compelled to rife through the box. I saw other clippings entitled: "David Nouveau Suddenly Disappears from Pop Music Scene" "Crystal Pegasus Tour Suddenly Cut Short— New Pop Music Star Disappears"

I dumped these clips over the photo of Carolyn.

Minutes later, Laura, my sweetheart, opened our apartment door. Her hair was long, brown and soft. Flowing in the wind. Her face was heart-shaped with full lips, and her eyes sparkled. Alive, intelligent and with keen wit, she was a delight in my life, and I loved her for it. Laura looked up the staircase as a Slinky walked down the stairs. The toy arrived at her feet.

"Okay, David," Laura said, smiling and picking up the toy.

She strode to the top of the stairs, paused and read a page of the book in her hand.

Stepping from my hiding place, I quickly took her hand, and we flowed into an embrace, dancing…

As we danced, my mind flowed into a flight of imagination. In my daydream, I saw Laura gliding in a royal purple, flowing dress. I saw my own arms, and knew I was wearing an elegant, black tuxedo. We gracefully danced below a golden chandelier. I dipped Laura who sensuously melted into me. Then, she turned playful and pinched my nose. I sent Laura outward, spinning her…

And Laura asked, "David, why are you acting so strange?"

Her question knocked me right back into reality. We completed our dance in the kitchen. Once again, the lack of sleep had gotten to me.

Then Laura saw drunk Mark on the floor of the other room. I could have kicked myself for not having closed a particular kitchen door. It would have been better if I had found a gentler way to break the news to her.

"Oh, that's new…" Laura said.

"Laura, I met him at the cemetery. His wife died." Mark had told me this in the bar.

"Oh, that's so sad. Is there something we can do to help? … Wait a minute, David, this is a *person*. Not another stray cat…"

"Laura, he needs help—"

A moment later, Laura walked over to Mark, and gently

placed a pillow under his head. I put a blanket over him. Laura and I stepped back and watched him sleeping. I had a flash impression of how we'd be looking down at our own baby someday. Our baby would be asleep and curled around her blanket in a crib. Laura and I gently, lovingly put our arms around each other. It was a tender moment. In his sleep, Mark burped.

The next morning, the glorious sunrise painted the clouds brilliant red and gold hues. A beautiful, haunting, romantic, music piece began as the numbers of my clock radio formed "6:00 AM."

Laura's legs were woven gently around mine. In a warm bath of orange, dawn sunlight, Laura and I embraced in our sleep. Laura's head rested on my left arm. Suddenly, I opened my eyes and groaned: "Ahhh!"

Startled, Laura woke up and reached to help me.

"We've got to stop waking up like this everyday!" she said.

Her leg had fallen "asleep," giving her the pins and needles discomfort. My arm had also fallen asleep under her head. I massaged her leg.

"Is your leg asleep, too? Are you okay?" I asked.

"Are you okay? You never told me what happened at the doctor yesterday...."

Laura's question sent me into a memory of what I endured the day before. I had gone to Dr. Stewart's office. Nurse Susan led me toward an examining room that was at the end of a small hallway.

"Lucy, I'm home!" I said entering the examining room. Nurse Susan smiled at my imitation of Ricky Ricardo of the "I Love Lucy" television show. I glanced at the Band-Aid on my leg. I was lucky, just a bruise and small cut. I would not mention it to the doctor.

At that moment, Nurse Susan gently closed the door behind me, and she walked about two yards over to the nurses' station, where Nurse Janice was organizing paperwork. The nurses didn't notice that my room's door opened on its own.

"Oh, did you hear? David Nouveau is out of remission," Nurse Susan said. I overheard her, and I felt my stomach clutch.

Nurse Janice said, "Oh, that's too bad. You know how it is with his form of cancer. They get so weak; they end up in a wheelchair. Then it's just a short walk—" Nurse Janice began.

"You mean, 'roll,'" Nurse Susan finished. And the nurses chuckled.

"—a short 'roll' to them being stuck in bed—then poof—dead." Nurse Janice said. I was having trouble breathing at this point.

"Yeah. Too bad about David Nouveau. I like him," Nurse Susan said.

"He's a nice one. A real change from a lot of them around here."

"And to top it off, David's got that cold-hearted Dr. Stewart who..." said Nurse Susan.

In answer, Dr. Stewart snatched the file folder on me out of Nurse Susan's hand, as he tore past in a rush. Then he entered the examining room with cold efficiency.

"Ah yes. David. Where's your, um, partner, Laura?" Dr. Stewart said. He towered over me. The bedside manner of the iceberg that sunk the Titanic.

"Didn't think we'd have to put her through the worry this time. Dr. Stewart, I haven't been sleeping well. I've been falling asleep during the day and—"

"Had that problem once in college. Just got up and scrubbed the kitchen floor. Then I was tired. Fixed it right up. Anyway, the tests are back. Look, David—there's no easy way to say this. So brace yourself. You're out of remission."

It was official. Not just a rumor. The room started spinning around me.

"I know this may be difficult for an athletic young man like you. You will have good days and bad days. Sometimes...suddenly, you'll be weak. You won't be able to walk. Then you might rally for a while. But I don't want to give you false hope. You have two months, maybe three," Dr. Stewart said simply.

"Can't we do something?"

"Sure. I'll put you on this new form of chemotherapy. Best medication really. It has a surprising little benefit—you won't lose your hair."

"Well, I—"

"Right—then." Dr. Stewart looked at his watch. "See you Thursday."

Dr. Stewart left quickly.

I looked downward—the only thing real was the floor. As finite as my short life.

"David? What did the doctor say?" Laura asked again—and her question kicked me out of my memory. Laura and I were still in bed together, waking up on the day after Dr. Stewart pronounced my death sentence.

"So what can I say? He said that I'm shooting blanks...the sperm count was low." I lied to her. I just couldn't tell her. Not then. Why? Why couldn't I tell her about being out of remission? Why couldn't I let her in?

"And..." she prompted me.

"So I drop the briefs –"

"That sounds like a good idea."

"And try boxers—"

"That has possibilities."

"It kind of makes things cooler..." Here I was talking about ways to increase my sperm count because Laura wanted a baby. I was trying to distract her from what Dr. Stewart really said about my physical condition.

"And that's it? Nothing else? That's all the doctor said?"

Instead of replying, I leaned back. My pillow fell out of the way so I hit my head on the wall. I grabbed the offending pillow, "Traitor!"

Shaking the pillow, I fell off the bed and landed with a thud, leaving my feet pointed straight up.

"Are you done?" Laura asked.

"Done in. Overdone. Over easy—"

"Definitely scrambled," she quipped. "What's with the bandage?" she asked, pointing to my leg.

"Just a scratch," I said.

She reached her hand over and helped me up onto the bed. I sat next to her and I said, "I'll do the boxers thing. I know that having a baby is important to you."

"Look, what really counts to me is that you keep on getting the check-ups and that you're healthy. I don't want to lose you." Laura's face trembled on that thought.

"We'll get through this; we always do," I said. This was our special phrase. It had got us through the last time I was out of remission. But now I was just saying it lightly. I took a breath then went on, "You know what's next..."

Laura looked at me intently.

"Well, after the boxers, there's the birthday suit."

"I don't mind," she said looking downward.

"You only have one thing on your mind—"

"Biology!" she said.

Laura and I lay backward, beginning one of our best lovemaking sessions ever.

An hour later, Laura looked, from the kitchen, through the open doorway and saw Mark, still asleep on the floor. I came around the corner with a water pistol with an attached figurine of a flying horse. I pressed the trigger, and water from the pistol splashed on Mark's forehead. He woke up...

"Uggh! Who the hell are you?!" he yelled.

Splash! Another squirt of water had hit Mark on the forehead. He roared and got up. I ran as the wings fell off the flying horse figurine. Laura laughed at our antics.

Later that morning, I sat at the breakfast table with Laura and Mark. I put down a cup that was imprinted with a face of a cartoon-like worried man.

"So how long have you put up with this guy?" Mark asked.

"Two years," Laura said.

"Under the same roof?" Mark asked.

"Six months," I said.

"Married?" he asked.

"No," Laura said, her voice dripping with frustration.

"Not married. Living together. How committed of you."

Laura and I chuckled.

Mark joined us in laughter.

"What is this, the Inquisition?" I asked.

"I'm curious. So shoot me—" Mark said.

With a gleam in my eye, I raised my water pistol with the flying horse on it.

"You put that down—don't you get water on my

interview clothes," Laura said. She gave me a look of "Hey buddy—stray animals, okay—water on my clothes and you cross the line."

"I get it. She's got an interview. But why did you wake me up?" Mark asked.

"You have some wheels?" I asked.

"A motorcycle," Mark said.

"Great!"

"Okay. I get it. On one condition. Give me the gun. Give me the gun and no one gets hurt."

I hesitated, and Mark grabbed the water pistol out of my hand. I offered Mark the wings that had fallen off the flying horse attached to the water pistol.

"Keep 'em," he said.

Mark, Laura, and I chuckled.

Minutes later, Mark drove his used, battered, rusty Honda Hawk motorcycle while I sat behind him. We zoomed up a hill near the San Francisco's Cliff House and near the edge. My eyes went wide in fear!

"Uhh. Mark, how 'bout not so close to the edge!" I said.

"Oh, you don't want me to do this!" Mark teased me by momentarily steering closer to the edge. Then, he backed off to a safer distance. I caught my breath—really unnerved due to the height of the cliff. We sped down the road.

Ten minutes later, Mark and I rode up in front of the Day Camp building.

"Okay. Hop off," Mark said.

I did a somersault off the back of the motorcycle.

Mark looked heavenward and said, "You couldn't just send locusts?"

Inside the day camp, Mark and I walked past a world map hanging on the wall. Affixed above the map was one of my paper-hang-glider homemade toys.

"What's that?" Mark asked.

"Me—hang-gliding. What I've always wanted to do." I threw the paper hang-glider.

"David—you're afraid of heights."

"I'm not afraid of heights—I'm afraid of you!" I said. Then, I walked off. "I'll be right back." I could feel it—the start of a coughing fit. I made it into the restroom. I just didn't want to reveal my illness to Mark at that time.

While I was coughing in the restroom, Mark looked at paintings by the day camp kids. My friend Jennifer walked out of a door and saw Mark. With an appreciative smile, she immediately took off her glasses and hid them in an inner pocket.

"See anything you like?" Jennifer said, arriving next to Mark. There was a hint in her voice.

"Yes. There's some good stuff here. What is this place?" Mark asked.

"A day camp for kids, ages 6 through 13."

"And David is here as a—"

"David's a counselor," Jennifer said.

"A counselor? No—no way." Mark accidentally hit the corkboard and a picture fell off and Jennifer caught it— Mark caught her hand, and they smiled.

Meanwhile, inside the restroom, I tried to compose myself but the coughing fit continued. I needed to get back out there, but I couldn't let them see me like this. I grasped the sink with both hands, leaning forward toward the mirror. Slowly, the coughing fit faded, and I was able to return to Laura and Mark.

"Oh, you two have met," I said.

"She tells me that you have them fooled here into thinking you're an adult," Mark said.

I raised a sock puppet and looked at it...

"Did you hear what he said?" I said to the puppet. I had the sock puppet kiss Mark.

"David, if you do that again, I'll kill you."

Comically, I rushed off in a mock panic.

"That worked. I'm Mark," he said.

"I'm Jennifer," she said with a sweet smile.

Looking over my shoulder, I saw them shake hands.

It was another time—another place with smoke swirling around me. Coughing, I was on my hands and knees. A wheelchair loomed behind me. Then it transformed into the Intruder that towered over me. The Intruder and I fought furiously. Sword and claw igniting sparks. But I faltered. I was losing! I swung my sword, but I saw Carolyn! Suddenly, the Intruder's midsection swallowed my sword. I was left without a weapon. A white flash and—

I opened my eyes. I was back to reality, having come out of my meditation session. Watching my progress was my therapist Adina. She was in her 50s with a gentle look of concern on her face. She gave me a warm hug.

"I saw you go deeper in this meditation," Adina said.

"I don't know if this is working anymore. I mean, we came up with the Intruder—for these meditation sessions—"

"To help you—"

"—fight the cancer," I finished the thought.

"Yes. You're doing the full medical treatment?" she asked.

"Yes, Adina. I'm doing the full medical process plus your sessions. Just like last time...but I don't know."

"During this meditation, what did you see?"

"The Intruder. . ."

"And . . ."

"Carolyn," I said.

"Tell me about that."

"Not much to say. Carolyn... Carolyn was my world. When we got married, it was.... Then she left. That's it."

"David, you're resisting."

"I don't know how to stop resisting."

"At least talk to Laura," my therapist said.

Chapter Two

A few days past and I even had another session with Adina, my therapist. I felt agitated so I took a walk. Soon, I paced back and forth in front of a pay phone. I was lucky enough to find one. At the time, I wasn't carrying a cell phone of my own. My intuition told me I needed to save up the money that would have gone into the monthly fee.

I took a breath, trying to pull in courage to tell Laura the truth about my being out of remission. Preparing to follow Adina's guidance, I grabbed the phone, deposited coins and dialed. When Laura answered, I said, "Hey, I got to tell you something. Saw the Doctor today and… And he said to keep going with the boxers, and we can—Oh, there's my bus. I'll see ya." I hung up the receiver. There was no bus—I had lied to Laura again! And I hated myself for it. I kicked over a garbage can.

Later that day, Jennifer and Mark stood in the hallway of

the day camp. Jennifer turned to Mark and said, "...I'm glad we could have lunch together."

Carolyn, my ex-wife, sped around a corner bringing her daughter Toni. Carolyn was willowy. But strong. A spirit warm like a glowing Yule fire. Her hair was black, shiny, short and tightly curled. Precise. Her face had a gentle nose, but a sharp chin. Being attentive to Toni, Carolyn accidentally bumped into Jennifer.

"Excuse me," Carolyn said.

"I'm sorry. Are you all right?" Jennifer said.

"Fine. I'm here to enroll my daughter. She's very excited," Carolyn said, looking with motherly affection to Toni.

Carolyn looked back to Jennifer and said, "Could you tell me what I have to do?"

"Yes. The office is down this hall. And take a left at the end," Jennifer said. As she pointed, Jennifer accidentally tapped Mark in the chest and took advantage of the moment by caressing his shoulder.

"A left at the end?" Carolyn said.

"Yes. I am sorry," Jennifer said, referring to their bumping into each other.

"Accidents happen," Carolyn said.

Jennifer watched Carolyn and Toni go down the hall.

After Carolyn and Toni turned the corner, Jennifer said to Mark. "Come on. Let's eat."

Jennifer gave Mark a sweet smile. They left the building.

A couple of blocks away, I rode my bicycle and did some jumps. Minutes later, I rode past a sign "Hilltop Italian Restaurant."

Inside the Italian restaurant, Jennifer glanced at a display that had candles floating on water. Then, her eyes returned to Mark who sat with her at a side table. Mark quietly clicked his zils.

"I'm glad you could make lunch today. David likes this place," Jennifer said. She smiled, seeing Mark quietly clicking the belly-dancing small cymbals worn on his fingertips. She didn't know they were called "zils."

"Oh," Mark said.

"What's that you're doing?" Jennifer asked.

Mark continued quietly clicking his zils.

"Just a zil part."

"For what? What's it for?" Jennifer asked, trying to get him to talk.

"What?" Mark asked.

"The zil pattern," Jennifer said.

"Oh—it's for one of David's songs. He's recording in my home studio. He wants to do a music album. Says that it's really important to do it right now."

"Do you like David's music?" Jennifer said.

"Well," Mark then changed topics: "Check this out." He tapped a beat.

"Which do you like better? This—" He tapped a beat.

"Or this?" He tapped a different beat.

"That the second one."

"I like the first one," Mark said.

"Well—they're both pretty good, but I prefer the second…"

Mark smiled, noticing that Jennifer stayed with her choice. He played the second part. He really got into it and started to get loud. Then both he and Jennifer looked up, and saw many of the restaurant patrons staring at them.

"O—kay," Mark said, a bit embarrassed.

Mark and Jennifer leaned in toward each other as Mark talked quietly. A moment of real connection for them.

Mark said, "You're right. The second pattern does have something. Uh...David's music is okay. It just needs some punch."

"Like your zil pattern."

"Yeah, like my zil pattern," Mark said, smiling warmly.

Jennifer returned his smile.

Mark stopped clicking his zils. Then, he absently fiddled with his ornate pin—like some guys might adjust a necktie.

"That's a nice pin," Jennifer said.

"Debbie gave me this for our wedding."

"You're married," Jennifer said. Her face dropped in deep disappointment.

"I was..." Resigned, Mark put the zils into a blue pouch and placed the pouch on the table.

The next morning, outside the day camp building, Jennifer ran up to Carolyn.

Jennifer said, "Mrs. Verdoux—thanks for coming so quickly after I called you on the phone."

"Toni's okay?"

"She seems fine. As I told you, it was a little accident."

Carolyn's face clenched in fear and concern for her daughter Toni.

Quickly, Jennifer opened the front door and guided Carolyn into the building.

Carolyn said, "You said little accident. What exactly happen?"

Jennifer took a breath and said, "Well—Toni slipped, hit her head—and fell into the swimming pool. Luckily one of the counselors was nearby, and dived in after her."

"Oh my God, is she all right? Where is she?" Carolyn asked.

"She's being examined by the camp doctor. I'll take you to

her…" Jennifer said.

Minutes later, Dr. Roberts and Toni exited his office door.

Jennifer led Carolyn up to the doctor and Toni.

"Oh, honey," Carolyn said as she quickly kneeled, looked Toni over, and gently hugged her.

"Dr. Roberts, This is Mrs. Verdoux, Toni's mother," Jennifer said.

"Is she all right?" Carolyn asked.

"Toni did have a bit of a fall. I've examined her. And other than a bump on her head, she's fine. She's made of strong stuff," Dr. Roberts said.

"Are you really all right?" Carolyn said to her daughter.

"No big deal, Mom. I'm okay."

"You're okay. Mommy's not." Carolyn turned to the doctor and thanked him.

Carolyn asked Jennifer: "May I thank the counselor who pulled Toni out of the pool?"

"Certainly. Come with me."

Carolyn looked to the doctor, who said, "Toni, how about we wait for your mom in my office?"

"Okay," Toni said.

Down the hall and around the corner was my day camp classroom. I was in between classes, and I held my ever-present paper hang-glider toy in my hand. I threw the hang-glider upward.

Jennifer and Carolyn entered the room and witnessed my playfulness.

Jennifer said, "Ms. Verdoux, I'd like you to meet—"

I turned around.

"David," Carolyn said in shock.

I was stunned, seeing my ex-wife. The hang-glider-man

floated past my face.

"Carolyn," I said.

"What are you doing here?" she asked.

"I work here. One of the kids fell—and I was waiting around to hear from the camp doctor."

"You're the one who saved her?" Carolyn asked.

"Yeah, I—. You're Toni's mom?"

"Have you been working here all along?" Carolyn asked.

"Well...it took me a while—"

"David, I mean, this summer?"

"Yes."

"You're kidding—what about your music?" Carolyn asked.

"Took a little break from the spotlight. Writing a lot." I took a breath. "Toni's a good kid. You're proud of her, huh?"

"She's a great kid. Yes, I am. Uh—she talked about David teaching music. But I had no idea that it was you."

"Uh—she's about six, right?" I asked.

"Yes. She just turned six."

"I guess it wasn't too long after we—after we—" I gestured with my hands showing our splitting apart. "—that you met someone."

"No, David, I'd rather not talk about that. I just want to thank you so much."

"Well, you're welcome."

Carolyn's cell phone rang.

"I have to take this," Carolyn said as she left the room.

A moment later, Jennifer went to the door and gave me a look that implied, "You've been holding out on me, buddy. You're going to tell me about this woman."

That afternoon, Mark and I walked outside his apartment

building. I could feel discomfort whirling in my chest like a tornado—all from seeing Carolyn. A punching bag hung on a pole in the backyard area.

"I feel like punching something. Can you hold this for me?" I asked.

Mark held the bag, and I punched the bag. I kicked it sending the bag and Mark to the floor. Comically, Mark's eyes grew wide from the impact to the ground as the bag pinned him down with his arms and legs dangling around it. His sunglasses were knocked askew, and his face grew red.

Mark asked, "Was it good for you?"

Minutes later, I practiced on the synthesizer keyboard in Mark's room that was home recording studio.

"Mark, thanks for your work on my album. You know, it's important to me. I'm so glad you have this home studio."

"Me, too...I think..." Mark said.

I sat near Mark who sat at his double synthesizer console. Mark's room was small with a multi-track tape recorder, four synthesizers, a baby electric grand piano, and two mixing boards with lights like Christmas tree lights. A modern art painting was tacked on the wall. A piece of toast was also tacked on the wall. I don't know why. He never told me. I folded a paper hang-glider toy—making a good luck charm for this recording session.

"So tell me about your daughter," Mark said.

"Not my daughter. My ex-wife's. Toni is Carolyn's daughter," I said.

"Uh-huh."

"Carolyn would have told me," I said.

"The girl's how old?"

"Six."

"And you split up—"

"Six years ago. I still don't see—"

"And isn't it strange that she just happens to look—Asian?"

"So what? Carolyn has a thing for Asians. Besides I have a problem."

"What problem?"

"A sperm count problem," I said.

"Sperm?"

"Sperm! Tadpoles! Making babies! I need some support here!"

"Okay, okay," Mark said. He paused, then continued, "You're sure they said sperm?—not marbles?"

"...no... No, that was years ago," I said.

At just that moment, Laura arrived at the door. I got up from the keyboard and gave her a warm hug.

"Hi there. Glad to see you. So what's up?"

"You didn't forget, did you?" Laura asked.

"No." I said.

"What didn't you forget?"

"Exactly what you're thinking about."

"And that is?"

"Why should I tell you?"

"We are going to..."

"To..."

"My..."

"Your..."

"Mother..."

"Mother's house! I'll drive," I said, taking Laura in my arms and rushing out the door.

Soon Laura wore a bicycle helmet, while I drove a shopping cart with her in it. We sped down a hill on the sidewalk. I had my feet on the shopping cart, and we were racing along. Laura smiled. We laughed and moved faster down the hill. Then I saw it: a car pulled out from a garage, blocking our path twenty five feet ahead. I jumped off and tried to stop the shopping cart, but my shoes were slipping on the cement. Laura was terrified, and she cringed. Twenty feet from the car, my feet continued to slide. Laura closed her eyes—

—Ten feet from the car,

—My feet slid,

—My face straining,

—Two feet,

—One...

Two inches before the car, I brought the shopping cart to a halt.

"You okay?" I asked.

"...yeah." she said. The driver gave us a disgruntled look and had his car roar off.

"Good," I said to Laura. Then, I noticed a young woman stepping from a photo-processing camera shop. Her face— the same woman who had slapped Mark at the cemetery. He'd just taken the slap, like he felt he deserved it. A photo slipped and fell from the young woman's folder. Unaware, she got in a car and drove away.

"Just a minute," I said to Laura. I jogged over to the camera shop and picked up the photo. I glanced at it and knew that Mark would be truly interested in this photo. But this was intense—when and how could I give the photo to him? Still pondering this conundrum, I stuck the photo into one of my jacket's pockets and returned to Laura.

"What was that?" Laura asked.

"Tell you later."

Then Laura's face lit up, and she said, "Oh! David, I

forgot to tell you about my dream last night."

"Yes?"

"I was at the park. You know the one we like to walk around?"

"Uh-huh."

"And this voice. It was...big. Like it was coming from everywhere at once. It said, 'Trust.'"

"Trust?"

She nodded.

"Did you write that in your journal?"

"Not yet... When I get home. Good idea."

In triumph, I stood, arms raised, like I was a successful Olympic athlete.

"Come here, you big ham."

We kissed.

Twenty minutes later, Laura stood at the top landing of a five-story wooden staircase that was attached to the back of her mother's apartment building.

Laura looked downward and called to me, "Come here. Come on."

My stomach wrenched with my terror of heights. I slowly stepped out of her mother's back doorway. I looked up to Laura who was one flight above me. I clutched the side of the building and barely inched forward. I said, "I think your mom is calling me."

"Come here, I want to show you..."

"I am close enough," I said.

"Come here."

"No, thank you."

"You're the one who dreams of flying."

"Flying is not falling," I said.

"This was my favorite spot when I was growing up. I

loved the sun, the quiet, the fresh breeze flowing on my face," Laura said.

I leaned toward her and said, "Okay, saw it!"

I ducked right back into the house.

Chapter Three

The next day, I stood before some day camp kids as I told a story. Carolyn's daughter, Toni, listened; her eyes wide with excitement.

"So while the other kids are at the swimming pool, we've got something to do. It's story time," I said.

"Story time! Story time! Cool!" kids said.

"And here's our main character," I said, drawing a horse on the white board.

"What's that look like?" I asked.

"New York," a girl said.

"A Chihuahua," a boy said.

"Something bigger." I said.

"A pony!" Toni said.

"Yes, Toni! It's a pony. Does this look like a pony?"

"No!" the kids said.

I mimed being knocked into the wall by the kid's exclamation.

"Well, it's a pony, okay!? Sniff—Sniff It's a pony!" I said.

The kids laughed. Toni pulled out a pen and paper and

started sketching a pony. In Toni's imagination, the pony turned its head and winked at her.

"And this pony was…"

"What's the pony's name?" Toni asked.

"De'mar. A nice pony, but nothing special until one night, while he was sleeping something happened. He woke up the next morning—and looked from side to side—and saw wings! He looked something like this!"

I did a magic trick and made my flying horse figurine appear out of thin air!

"Ooooo!" the kids said.

I did another magic trick and made the figurine disappear!

"Oh! Where'd it go?!" a boy said.

Then I continued the story: "Soon the barnyard animals talked heatedly. They did not like that De'mar had new wings. They wanted to find the creature who gave De'mar the wings and give them back. This scared De'mar. What would they do to him? Would they cut them off? De'mar ran away, and the other animals chased after him. Faster, and faster he ran, and faster and faster the other animals chased. Then, WHOOSH, De'mar took off into the air! This was cool! So here was David flying along—"

"De'mar!" The kids said.

"What?"

"His name is De'mar!"

"You said David!"

"Oh. Right! So De'mar flew higher and higher. He flew until the barnyard animals could no longer reach him. He really liked flying. Never again, he thought, would he return to the barnyard... After a while, the sun went down. He looked at the stars, looked at the moon, didn't see the tree—"

WAP! I slapped the back of my hand to my forehead—showing the branch hit, and said, "OW!"

In her mind's eye, Toni imagined a cartoon flying pony hitting his head and his eyes going cross!

The kids laughed.

"So he fell," I said, adding a whistling sound—the sound of the falling pony.

Toni eyes went wide.

"And landed on—"

The kids called out, "Clouds! Hay! A Bachelor cake with a girl popping out!"

"He fell on clouds that felt like hay and bounced onto a bachelor cake and landed in the Enchanted Lake."

Toni imagined the cartoon pony falling into the lake with a big splash.

"De'mar swims to the shore, but this made him really tired so he fell asleep. The next morning, he woke up—'Hah! You're the weirdest thing I've ever seen,' said the Mocking Bird. De'mar looked at his hooves and his wings and saw he had changed again. He was made of Crystal!"

"Crystal?" Toni asked.

"Yes, like really nice glass." I said. "So De'mar was now a 'Crystal Pegasus.'"

"Crystal Pegasus!" Toni said.

"Yes. The Mocking Bird said, 'You know, crystal can't fly. You'll break. You're glass.'"

"De'mar replied, "Wait-wait. If I flap my wings like this—" I whacked my hand on the wall, miming De'mar's wing. "OWWW!" I jumped around and blew on my hand to soothe it. On cue, the kids laughed.

"So Crystal Pegasus just moped around until he heard..."

At that moment, Jennifer stepped over to me. She was in a cute Owl costume—with a beak-nose and some feathers. Her face was in a scowl showing that she felt silly.

"Who. Who are you?" Jennifer said.

"Said the Wise Owl," I explained.

Frowning, flapping her hands, Jennifer said, "Why are you hiding under this tree?"

Portraying Crystal Pegasus, I replied, "Everybody is laughing at me."

"Why don't you just fly away?"

"Can't fly away. I'm made of crystal."

"So?"

"The Mocking Bird told me."

"You believed a Mocking Bird? Look, all you need to do is climb to the top of that mountain over there. And...Jump off!" Her eyes and tone gave me a jab.

"What?!"

"Sure. It works all the time. You just go to the highest cliff because it'll take you a while to get it right—ON THE WAY DOWN." Another jab at me.

"But I don't want to—"

"Yes, you do," Jennifer said.

"No."

"Come on. I'll show you. I'll meet you at the top."

"And the Wise Owl flew off. And Crystal Pegasus didn't go up there for—two days. But finally, Crystal Pegasus climbed up the mountain. Until, at last, he was at the edge of the cliff."

"Now—jump off!" Jennifer said.

"'Uh—Uh'" said Crystal Pegasus as he just stood there, trying to work up his courage..."

Toni sat entranced. In her imagination, she saw a cartoon Crystal Pegasus standing on top of the cliff—scared and shaking his head 'no' as the Wise Owl looked on, disgruntled.

Jennifer's cell phone rang.

"Hello," Jennifer said. "Yes, I'll tell him." She turned to me. "David, your lunch appointment is here. You'll need these." She handed me two toy swords and pointed their tips at my face.

Pretending to be timid, I said, "Thanks…"

Some minutes later, Laura and I crossed toy swords—on a hill above a park. I caught a glimpse of the gorgeous view of downtown San Francisco with the distinctive Transamerica pyramid building. Laura jabbed me in the butt! She ran laughing as I pursued her. She leapt on the deck of a playground boat holding her sword at guard, keeping me at bay. In a grand gesture, I tossed my sword away, surrendering to her unconditionally, and in turn, she tossed her sword to the ground. I held out my hand and stood like a master dancer. Laura glided into my arms, and we danced. We twirled, and the sounds of kids playing in the playground faded away. It was just Laura and me.

That evening while Laura was revising her resume, I returned to Mark's place. I let myself in because I knew where he kept his spare key. Inside his studio-room, I found a videotape. I became curious and placed it in Mark's VCR. The tape played, and there was Mark with a woman— dancing. They swirled around and around. She moved with entrancing grace, her long auburn hair flowing in a light breeze.

Mark clicked his zils and the small instruments were caught in a couple of well-placed close-ups.

With San Francisco Bay a glorious, sunbathed blue in the background, Mark and the woman flowed through breathtaking choreography. Joy filled their faces as they gracefully moved in unison. I became intrigued by the way their eyes met each other as they danced. Clearly, they were in love.

Mark arrived at the doorway of the room. He said nothing and the room became pregnant with silence as the tape played. Then he gruffly cleared his throat—a feral growl. Like a tornado, Mark furiously thrashed about. He yelled and screamed at me, and his eyes filled with terrible rage. Startled, I stumbled over my words, as I frantically thought about what to say, and then it was all over. Mark grew silent again, though his breath was heavy. Sweat poured down his face.

Silence marked by the strained breathing filled the room.

"Get out!" Mark roared.

I did not hesitate. Quickly, I left the room, and as I closed his front door, I paused and looked back. I should have just waited. I should have asked him about that tape before I ever thought about putting it in his VCR to play it. But I had let my curiosity overrun my thinking. I felt as though I had been punched in the gut, and it was my own fault.

That night, sitting in our apartment, Laura listened to our answering machine.

She heard a bored woman's voice saying: "...I'm sorry the position for assistant professor has been filled."

I entered and leapt on the couch near Laura. Seeing her eyes, I quieted down.

She said, "I lost the Kerwin job. Damn it! I'm tired of temp jobs; they're supposed to be temporary! I'm a trained biologist—this is a waste of material! And it's a waste of time!"

"What's this?" I asked, grabbing a letter that Laura was using as a bookmark. The letter turned out to be just a form rejection letter.

"They missed their chance! You know, it's gonna be one lucky biology lab that hires you," I said.

I gave her a hug, "We'll get through this; we always do," I said, repeating our phrase. The words that we always told each other. To remind us that we were flowing with life. And that we could count on being together.

"Something I could do to help?" I asked.

Laura nodded toward her back. I understood and moved behind her. I turned on our small boom box, and as the music played, I placed my hand on the crest of her shoulders and slowly began to rub. I could feel the tension in her neck as my thumbs pressed deeply into the muscle. Slowly, meditatively I closed my eyes to concentrate.

I was riding the soaring Crystal Pegasus. He was fully-grown, and the office buildings of San Francisco reflected on his crystalline body. It had to be a dream. But it felt so real. Although Crystal Pegasus looked like ice, he was warm, and I felt safe riding him.

Crystal Pegasus and I flew near the summit point of the Transamerica building. Then, he came down for a landing in Union Square.

Then images blended. His wing flowed back…and I saw a sunrise. And in moments, I felt an urgency to find Toni. For some reason, I felt that she was in danger. I hopped off Crystal Pegasus' back and looked for the little girl. Half a block away, I saw the Intruder. Its arms raised then lowered leaving the shadows of five hoodlums. I watched the hoodlums with concern. Eerily, the hoodlums turned in unison and stared to the left. I followed their gaze and saw little Toni, who looked vulnerable in her pink party dress. I leapt up, swung on a tree branch and landed in front of the hoodlums—blocking their path to Toni. Using the karate skills I had gained as a child, I kicked two bad guys into unconsciousness.

My foot in his groin, then my knee in his head felled another attacker. I slammed my palm in the face of another hoodlum. Then I faced the biggest bad guy. His first punch sent me down. He waited for me to rise. I used a wall to support me. Then we traded blows. My elbow then my crescent kick knocked him to the ground. I heard clapping—it was Laura.

A few feet away, Carolyn smiled at me and said, "Thank you, please be my daughter's godfather."

I smiled. Suddenly, from the ground, the biggest bad guy kicked me in the chest—

I woke up, pain in my chest, knocked right out of my dream. The flare of a small bright lamp making me wince, I realized that I had dozed off while working on a song. I crumpled the paper I was writing on and threw the paper ball into the wastebasket. I turned and saw Laura still sleeping in our bed. I stifled a cough, trying to hide it, and not wake up Laura.

The next day, I jogged along a street near the San Francisco Bay. Sweating profusely, I felt overwhelmingly tired. My illness was acting like a crushing weight, and I had to stop. And still, my thoughts swirled. What could I do to smooth things with Mark? What about my illness and confiding in Laura?

I looked at my watch. "What? Only twenty minutes?" I was gasping for air.

"I thought I recognized you!"

I turned my head to see Trudy, the elderly woman in her wheelchair—the person I had saved from the car. She gave me a warm smile. I smiled in return, still catching my breath.

"Oh. . . Hello," I said. I couldn't hold my smile.

"Something's bothering you. You want to tell Aunt Trudy about it?"

"Uh...I...my name's..."

"David Nouveau."

"How did—?" I asked.

Trudy held up an audio CD that read "David Nouveau—Crystal Pegasus."

She said, "You have a gift. I asked at the music store. You haven't released an album in years..."

I was silent.

"You've got to live your dreams." She smiled. "Look at me. I've always wanted to live in this city. *And here I am.*"

I felt a smile play on my face. I kneeled so that I was at her eye level. "Trudy, I'm back in the studio. In fact, I've got to wash up and go there now."

"Glad to hear it."

I gave her hand a friendly squeeze, and turned to go.

"Oh, David..."

Trudy pulled out a red rose and handed it to me. I started to reach for it. But I hesitated; I couldn't accept the rose. It was gift. But something inside me shut down at its presentation. In a forced moment, I took hold of the rose and smiled, masking my unease.

"Thanks. I'll see you."

I walked away.

"Be good to yourself," Trudy said.

Without turning, I lifted my hand, acknowledging her comment. I walked around the corner. As soon as I was out of Trudy's sight, my hand dropped, letting the rose fall.

That afternoon, in front of the day camp, Jennifer watched as Carolyn kneeled down to Toni. Carolyn handed a cellular phone to Toni.

"Toni, you can use this to call me," Carolyn said.

"Okay, Mom." Toni hugged Carolyn. Full of energy, Toni

rushed from her mother, grabbed Jennifer's hand and jerked Jennifer toward the day camp building. Pulled along, Jennifer smiled wanly and waved goodbye to Carolyn.

That afternoon, I sat drawing, waiting in the day camp patio. It was my afternoon break time. Toni ran in and jumped on my lap!

"What's that?!" she asked.

I handed it to her, and Toni held it reverently.

"Oh. It's Crystal Pegasus! Could I learn to draw it that way?"

"Sure!" I said, smiling. "Keep it."

"Thanks! Bounce me high!

I lifted Toni—"bouncing her."

"Higher! Higher!" she said.

It was a joy to make Toni happy.

Two hours after my day camp workday was done, Mark and I walked in a park on the way to his home.

"Hey, I'm—I'm sorry about playing the tape—" I began.

"It's done," Mark said, tightly.

"I don't know how it happened. I mean: I want to be respectful and—"

"Then be respectful. I don't want to talk about it." He closed the subject.

We walked in silence.

The tension was killing me. I saw an opportunity to shift the mood: I playfully walked on a crack in the cement like it was a tightrope. I carried my backpack in my right hand.

Mark played along and tossed in a playful-exasperated comment: "I don't even know why I agreed to do this CD album with you."

"Because you like this shade of green." I held out two $20

bills. So that's why my intuition said to save the money I would have paid for a cell phone-monthly fee.

Just as Mark reached for the two bills, I playfully pulled them back.

Mark brightened and said, "I've got some news. Jennifer needs me—"

"Good!"

"—to help her move tomorrow."

"Bad! Did you tell her we have a session?" I asked.

"Yes. But someone cancelled on her, and she's hit the deadline."

"You're going—"

"I'm sorry," Mark said.

"What about tomorrow night?"

"Didn't you promise to do something for Laura then?"

"What about tomorrow night?"

"It's only one day. What's the fuss? We'll pick it up Thursday," Mark said.

I almost confided in him, *"I have to finish this album in 2 months because I'm out of remission."* But I switched the subject and said, "That's it!"

"What?" Mark asked.

"I just got it."

"Oh no…" Mark said.

I ran over to and climbed up a large bell. A landmark in the park.

"You don't appreciate the grand gesture!" I said.

"And this album—"

"—is my grand gesture. To leave something behind that's worthwhile and beautiful. I want to feel like I'm really living! I want to SOAR!"

"—into the sky and down into a straight jacket!" Mark said.

"I heard that!" I said, climbing down from the bell. "You're sure you can't work tomorrow?"

"Yeah."

"It's just taking so long. All the retakes..." I said.

"David, I said I would help you. And I will." I could feel his sincerity. His help was something I could count on.

"Okay," I said with a sigh. "Well, you better or—" I said as I reached into my backpack—but didn't find what I was looking for. With a triumphant smile, Mark held up the water pistol and said, "Looking for this?!"

I ran. Mark aimed. His shot of water caught me in the rear.

Twenty minutes later, in his home studio, I turned to Mark who was untangling a "spaghetti" of wires.

"...so that's when Adina talked to me about rituals," I said.

Absorbed in his untangling task, Mark paid little attention.

"Uh-huh. What kind of ritual?" he asked.

"It could be just about anything. Some people light a candle and relax in a hot bath... I was thinking of going primal with mine. Yeah, we'll have thirty cheerleaders with antlers on their heads. With beef hotdogs. We'll have shish kabob. Then, we'll drink testosterone..."

"Uh-huh."

"Drums, shrunken heads, sacrificial victims—are you volunteering?"

"op—sure," Mark said, still distracted.

"Good. I'll meet you at 7. You bring the white robe. I'll bring the dagger."

I was smiling, joking. Finally Mark caught on.

He said, "I have just one thing to say to you... 'therapy.'"

"I'm in it," I said.

"Then I have something else to say... 'more.'"

Chapter Four

That afternoon, Mark and I took a break from recording my CD album, and met Jennifer and Laura at the park. Between us, Mark and I carried a plastic bucket of items: a football, toy swords, and other things. For the fun of it, we two couples did some playacting and skits. Mark and Jennifer walked along next to the jungle gym. Leaping and landing near the couple, Laura and I brandished two toy swords. Mark stepped forward in front of Jennifer to defend her. He swung out his own weapon—a plunger. Mark and I plunged into a comical swordfight with gusto!

Next, I threw a football to Laura who threw it to Jennifer who threw the football to Mark. He nonchalantly raised a plastic garbage bucket. The football smoothly glided into it! Mark looked on with evident dignity.

Finally, Laura engaged in a toy swords duel with Mark. She won by jabbing Mark in the stomach with her fuzzy-sword. He dropped his sword and keeled over with big overacting gestures. Jennifer retrieved Mark's fallen sword to battle for his honor. But Laura won again, jabbing Jennifer this time with her toy sword. Jennifer keeled over but made sure that she pretended to die with her head, sweetly on Mark's shoulder.

Laura nudged me in the ribs in the manner of "Hey, will you look at that; they're becoming a couple."

About an hour later, Mark and I walked down a street, lined with eucalyptus trees.

"What do you think they're doing?" I asked Mark.

"Who?

"Laura and Jennifer," I said.

"Don't know."

"If we're lucky, they're doing and planning something diabolical," I said playfully.

"Right."

"Sure. I have hidden depths. Dark, deep mysteries. Like..." I pulled out my soap bubble bottle and blew soap bubbles into Mark's face.

"That's you, David. Evil incarnate!"

We walked for a moment.

"All right, so give me the scoop. What do you think of her?" I asked.

"Who?"

"Jennifer!"

Mark took a breath and said, "Jennifer's a very sweet lady. But...the truth is I get the feeling she wants something that I...can't give anymore."

I opened my mouth to say something, but then bit my lip. Suddenly, Mark walked off. I hesitated. I thought that maybe I needed to let Mark have time to himself. But I was concerned. I changed my mind and walked toward Mark.

It was a typical cold San Francisco day that reminded me of the quote "The coldest winter I ever spent was a summer in San Francisco." So I stuck my hands in my jacket pockets. But then I felt something in one pocket, and I pulled out a photo. It was the photo the woman had dropped in front of the camera shop. I looked at the photo intently and made a snap decision. I quietly walked to Mark, placed the photo in front of him, and stepped away. Mark looked down and grabbed the photo: it was of Mark and Debbie, his deceased wife, at their wedding reception. Their faces glowed with joy. Mark was dashing in his tuxedo, and Debbie was angelic in her wedding dress.

Mark shook and then sobbed with anguish.

What could I do? I just stood some distance away and watched him cry. I hoped that if he could express the anguish and get it out of his system—that he could eventually heal. I felt a tug on my soul as Mark cried. Maybe if I helped Mark—somehow I could heal, too.

About an hour later, we made it back to Mark's home studio. We didn't say anything. We just got started working again. I played music on a keyboard, and when I finished, I looked over at Mark cueing him to stop the recording. Mark, however, didn't see me. He was distracted and the tape continued to record.

"Mark....yo!"

"Oh...yeah," Mark said as he turned the tape deck off.

"Do you need a break?

"No, I was just thinking," Mark said.

"About what?"

"Don't cross-examine me."

"Sorry," I said.

We were quiet for a moment. Finally, Mark said quietly, "I was looking at the wheels going around. I was thinking of wheels. Remember that woman who slapped me? That's

Debbie's sister."

"Mm-hmm."

"Have you ever seen me—? Well, now, you've seen me drunk. Ever seen me high?"

"No," I said.

"I only got high once. When Debbie and I got married, we had a reception. The band got us an ice cream cake." He smiled and went on. "Debbie looked like an angel. Later, there was this pipe, being passed around. I thought it was just pot, so I took a drag. We weren't leaving for a couple of hours. I remember thinking, 'Wow, this is really strong.' It must have been laced with something."

Mark took a breath. "So a few hours later, I'm driving us down to Santa Cruz. Feeling fine. Just fine. Happy like nothing could go wrong. I should have had no trouble. All I had to do was swerve… And…"

Mark's eyes tensed as he saw the horror of that night… "Debbie!"

I watched, concerned.

"You never asked. That's what happened," he said.

I sat there, listening as Mark told me about his beloved Debbie. The one woman who really got him, understood him, listened to him at midnight even though she was a morning person. The one woman who knew just when to massage his neck and just when to stop. Debbie. Mark cherished her so much that he forced himself to go to bed at 9 PM, and he would lay there every night for thirty minutes until she was asleep. She had told him that she really loved to fall asleep near him. He would lay still for her. He felt honored to do that. To be so lucky to have a life with her. But now he didn't have that life. Only memories. It was like she was on the other side of bulletproof glass. He could never hold her again.

The next morning, I walked into the empty kitchen. I looked around for Laura. Where was she? Then I got this weird thought and I ran over to the top of our staircase. I looked down and found Laura in a crumpled heap at the bottom of the stairs. Was she dead?! I ran to her.

"Laura!" I called out.

I started to feel for a pulse...

"Boo!" Laura said.

I became furious and ran up the stairs.

"You're just upset that you bought it—that I got you this time," Laura said.

She found me in the living room. I was so upset that I was shaking.

"It was just a joke," she said.

"A joke—Ha, Ha," I oozed sarcasm.

"I'm sorry," Laura said, puzzled.

"...okay." I took a breath. Laura was precious to me. I loved her with all my heart. I felt so blessed to be with her. I would do whatever it took to break my bad mood, and do something good for her. I reached up, brought down a box, and gave her the box. She opened it to find a painting of us riding Crystal Pegasus. I had painted us soaring into a night sky of stars. Then I opened a "Happy Birthday" sign that was a bright rainbow of colors.

"It's beautiful. Thank you," Laura said.

The following morning, I felt some energy return and decided to ride my bicycle. With my flute in my vinyl quiver on my back, I rode past a cable car as it crossed in front of the Transamerica Pyramid Building that was visible in the distance. I even did a couple of bicycle stunts, hopping onto a cement banister. I raced down the sidewalk.

Suddenly, an empty wheelchair zoomed in front of me,

and my front wheel slammed into it. I plunged into the cement sidewalk!

I opened my eyes as I stepped out of my meditation. The crash had been in my mind. My therapist Adina was leading me into a meditation exercise to reconnect with my healthy and energetic feelings. Somehow, my inner turmoil had sabotaged the whole thing. I saw a frown come upon Adina's caring face.

"What happened?" she asked.

"It's not going away this time," I said. Adina decided to switch her whole approach and brought me into her kitchen. She said, "What do you want?"

"For lunch?" I asked.

"That's a start. Pasta or tofu burgers?"

"Pasta."

"What do you really want?" Adina asked.

"I want the pain to stop."

"What comes to your mind when I say 'forgiveness?'"

I frowned.

"Let's try another way to look at it. Let's say that this—" She held up a bowl of pasta and water. "—is a human being."

"Pasta and water?" I asked.

"Go with me a bit. Just suppose you could be in the moment, and let all the anger, guilt feelings, and the past just drain away."

Adina placed the pasta into a strainer, and the water flowed out. It drained into the sink.

Chapter Five

That afternoon, I met Trudy near the Bay Bridge. The blue water of the Bay glistened in the sun. Mark had told me before that the bay was not blue. But that particular day, it was blue. It suited my meeting with Trudy. In some way, Trudy was more than another therapist to me. She helped me as a spiritual guide in her wheelchair. I felt it was important for me to talk with her again. So I waited earlier in the day at the corner where we first met. From there our connection grew.

"So tell me about Laura," Trudy said.

"Where do I start? I mean, she's funny. She's kind. She thinks I'm funny. I really love her."

"How'd you meet?"

"It was at a workshop: 'How to Flirt.'"

Trudy laughed and said, "Don't tell me you didn't know how."

"Well . . . I'm always looking to learn things."

"Bet you two showed everybody in the class how to flirt."

I laughed. "Yes. I guess we did."

My eyes fell onto Trudy's wheelchair. In response, she spun her wheelchair, using her hands. I looked on and thought, "Here we go again."

"Look alive!" Trudy said.

Trudy did another spin and as she completed the turn, she caught her breath and said, "Good! Not as good as a roller coaster, but good. I haven't been on a coaster in... years."

"That's something I can fix," I said and pushed Trudy down the sidewalk quickly. We zoomed around some benches near the San Francisco Bay. We laughed. I pushed Trudy so fast that the rubber of one wheel fell off. It took me a half hour to get it back on. But it was worth it. Trudy's smile and the exhilaration on her face were priceless.

That afternoon near a park, Mark and Jennifer walked happily along and recited poems that they both loved. They said in unison, "And the glory that was Rome." They walked on a bridge over streetcar tracks. Mark finally opened up and told Jennifer what was weighing heavily on his heart.

He finished by saying, "So that's what happened...that's how Debbie died." Remembering his wife's death shook Mark to the core. He stopped walking and turned to Jennifer.

"I'm sorry—" Mark said.

"But—but—we could—" Jennifer reached to Mark, but he grabbed her hands.

"Listen to me, listen to me! I—I am sorry."

Mark quickly walked away from her as a the streetcar roared beneath the bridge.

That evening, Mark and I were in his home recording

studio. I finished recording a take, and Mark was looking into space.

"So you finally have a defense mechanism against my music," I said.

"What? —oh, heh," Mark said.

A pause.

"I can't keep going on like this. Nothing's going to change," Mark said.

I was quiet, listening.

Mark looked me in the eye and said, "So what the hell was that ritual idea again?" I felt the spark of hope: Mark was asking about how to heal.

The next morning, Laura and I were poking around in our attic. Laura put some photographic solution bottles in a crate.

"I've found what I was looking for," Laura called out to me. She moved the crate and noticed the wheelchair, which I had used the last time I was out of remission from the cancer. "Oh, this is still here? David, how about you give this to the Salvation Army?"

She walked off, and I ran up, reaching for the wheelchair. My body tensed. Instead of grabbing hold of the wheelchair, I just clenched my hands into fists. I walked away from the wheelchair, leaving it untouched.

In the hallway, I coughed, and Dr. Stewart's business card dropped from my shirt pocket. I heard his voice in my mind, "David, if you cough up blood, have Laura take you to the hospital immediately. You could be near death."

Tom Marcoux

72

Chapter Six

After working at the day camp, I walked past the bushes near the place I had met Trudy and near the spot where my shoe had flown. The afternoon sun beat down on cemetery's gravestones, visible through a couple of gaps in the bushes.

I glanced about and saw the back of Trudy as she sat in her wheelchair. The wheelchair rolled on its own toward the street, and Trudy made no move to stop her wheelchair's straying. Concerned, I ran over to her and stopped the wheelchair just as one of the front wheels was poised in the air, about to tumble over the curb.

I locked the brakes on the wheelchair. Baffled, I looked at Trudy and saw that the elderly woman was dead. Perhaps, her heart had simply stopped.

Horror-stricken, I backed away from the face of death. Four people gathered around Trudy, taking over the situation.

"Call 911," one man said.

While another man dialed 911, the air seemed deprived of oxygen. *Hard to breathe.* I backed away from the scene, leaving the dear woman's body to the authorities. I ran.

At a pay phone, I frantically placed coins into the machine and dialed quickly. The phone rang while I rehearsed: "Laura, I'm out of remission. I'm getting treatment again. It's—"

The telephone stopped ringing as the "click" of the answering machine engaged. My own voice said: "Hello, David and Laura aren't near the phone right now. Please leave your message."

At that moment, I remembered that Laura was out on a job interview. . .

The phone answering machine went "beep." I said, "Uh. Hi, Laura. I was thinking of you. I know you're at your job interview. Uh. Good energy to you. Here's a prayer for everything to turn out well. See ya." I hung up, and my face dropped from the false smile and energy I'd given to leaving my message.

Frantic again, I reached into my pocket for coins and dropped them on the ground. I awkwardly put them into the phone. The phone rang as I said, "Come on. Come on!"

I heard Adina pick up her phone, and I said, "Adina, this is David!"

Twenty minutes later, in Adina's backyard, I sat in a chair near her.

"I just can't go back to the wheelchair. I can't get so weak that I can't walk," I said.

Adina tossed a bicycle helmet into my lap.

In Adina's driveway, I rode her nephew's bicycle in a circle as she stood in the center.

"How are you feeling?" she asked.

"Great. Free!"

"And how would you feel in the wheelchair?" Adina asked.

"Confined."

"That's just a thought in your mind, David. Just imagine that you could feel this freedom again. Anytime. You could feel grace in the moment," Adina said.

The next day, I walked down the sidewalk, carrying two grocery bags. Laura would be pleased that I took over the groceries chore this time.

I sat down on a bench to rest a bit. *Sleepy.* My head nodded and I was plunged into a nightmare.

My eyes snapped open. I was thrown about in the basket of a runaway shopping cart, racing down a hill. I got up, trying to escape. Something slammed into the cart. Knocked off my feet, I glanced back and saw a large Black Car. The vehicle raced up. Soon it would ram me again.

I glanced about in desperation then saw that the shopping cart had transformed into a wheelchair. Now my arms were tied to the armrests of the wheelchair!

Wham!—again the Black Car rammed me. My wheelchair zoomed down the hill toward an intersection with racing cars, back and forth. Death was ahead and behind me, too.

I pulled and somehow got my right arm free of the binding. I plunged my hand in my pocket, pulled out my Swiss Army knife.

I used my bound hand to hold the knife, and with my free hand I opened the knife. I cut the cord that bound my left arm, closed the knife and replaced it in my pocket.

Crouched on the racing wheelchair I prepared and leapt into the air.

I caught myself by grabbing a fire escape overhead. I agilely landed on the sidewalk and noticed that the wheelchair and the ominous Black Car were gone. I caught my breath, and a smile graced my face. I had survived!

I woke from the nightmare or *dream*. This one had turned out well!

I picked up the grocery bags and started crossing the street.

A Black Car came to a screeching stop near me. Startled, I tossed the grocery bags, and rolls of toilet paper went flying over my head—startling a businessman, who was walking near me. A young woman with a kind face put her head out of the driver's side window…

"Are you all right?" she asked.

I caught my breath. My heart still beating with terror.

That afternoon, I held a private piano lesson for Toni. She sat on my lap while I taught her the appropriate fingering on the electronic piano.

Carolyn tiptoed into the room. I motioned to Carolyn, inviting her to stay quiet while Toni played.

"Honey, that sounds great," Carolyn said to her daughter.

Then, Laura walked into the room. She was awkward.

"Piano lessons," I explained to Laura.

"David, you've done wonders with Toni," Carolyn said.

"You must be Carolyn," Laura said.

"And you're Laura," Carolyn replied, remembering the time I had said, "I can't do a lesson for Toni this Thursday; I'm already booked to do something with Laura—my sweetheart."

The two women were stiff, and I felt their discomfort toward each other. Laura broke the stalemate by kneeling down, to speak with Toni.

"Hi, Toni. What are you playing?"

"Peter, The Pumpkin Eater," Toni said.

"Sounds good," Laura said.

Carried by the music, Toni played the electronic piano and didn't notice the tension between Laura and Carolyn.

Thirty minutes later, Adina and I stood, facing each other in her backyard.

"You're resisting," Adina said.

"I told you. I don't know how to stop resisting," I said.

"Do one of your karate punches," Adina said.

I hesitated. Adina was using this ploy to get my attention. From other sessions, she knew that I had studied karate as a child. I had also taken a special self-defense class in which students strike full-force on a teacher in a heavily padded suit.

In fact, I had done some volunteer work for an organization that provided classes for women in this form of full-force, rape prevention training. Because I was an advocate for women, I still hesitated to throw a karate punch toward Adina. But she insisted.

I did a karate open-hand strike, and Adina blocked the strike. It stung.

"That's when force meets force. Try another punch."

I punched and this time Adina used Aikido, flowing out of the way and pulling me to the ground.

With my face in the grass, I said, "So what am I learning here?"

I got up and brushed some grass off me.

"We've talked about what you resist, persists. Now, I've shown you another way," Adina said.

"Okay, another way. Couldn't you have just—SPFFF—told me that?" I asked, spitting out grass.

"I go with my guidance in the moment," Adina said with a smile.

The next day, at his home, Mark told me, "Trust me. You'll feel better after this break."

Mark walked in and sat down on the couch.

I saw my chance to startle him, ran up and tossed myself onto the couch. There wasn't much room so my feet slammed onto Mark's lap. I smiled and relaxed; we were taking a break from the music production. Mark tossed my feet off his lap, and I went tumbling to the floor.

"That went better than expected," Mark said.

I gave Mark a disgruntled look. Then, I got an idea and jumped to my feet.

"Get up! Get up! I want to show you something. Come at me with a punch," I said.

"I don't think..."

"Don't worry. Adina showed me a move."

"Adina?" Mark asked.

"My therapist."

"Your therapist wants me to punch you...that makes sense."

Mark swung his fist and—

As a result of the blow that I failed to block I was a dazed heap on a chair.

"Is that your tooth?" Mark asked.

I grunted.

That night Laura woke up. She noticed that the clock read 4 AM. She felt the empty space next to her.

"David?"

Laura got up, walked to the kitchen and discovered me, wearing headphones and playing the little electronic piano. My eyes had days of little sleep rings under them.

"David." No response. She touched my shoulder. "David."

"WHAT?!" I yelled with exhausted anger.

"Nothing!" she said, profound hurt on her face.

She left me alone. I continued struggling with my music. I slammed my fist down on the electronic piano—creating a horrible discordant sound.

Chapter Seven

The next day I walked, my body hunched over with fatigue from my illness and my twisted feelings pressing down on me. Behind me was a building crafted to look like furniture was falling out of its windows. This building was a San Francisco landmark on 6th Street, a street marred by trash and grime. A building falling apart, like me—a sign of the times.

A week later, on a moonless night, Laura opened the refrigerator; it was empty. She shut the refrigerator door, and the kitchen fell to near-total darkness. Only my small light illuminated my paper for writing music notes. I stumbled over chords on the electronic piano, trying to write a song. As my nighttime studio, the kitchen oppressed me as a nightmare filled with my frustration, failing at music.

Laura pulled the plug of my headphones out of the electronic piano.

"David, we've got to talk. You promised to get groceries on your way back from the session," Laura said; anger turned her voice harsh.

Frustrated with each wrong chord that I played, I didn't look up.

"I'm busy. Would you just take care of it?"

"David, look we both gotta eat. I've been picking up after you for weeks."

I said nothing.

"This CD...I don't know...maybe it's not the time for it. I mean, you're snapping at me a lot now. That's not like you. You're not the same man—"

"That's right, I'm under pressure now."

"Then, let's talk about it—find a way—"

"Here's the way; let me do what I have to do," I said.

"You have more to do than just your CD. We got a life here together! I want a life partner. And I don't want to be a servant."

"So what are you telling me? You don't want to be supportive?"

"I've been nothing but supportive. There's a limit."

"A limit? The hell with you and your limits! I need you now. I need support now!"

"I've been there for you every minute. Helping you with the CD. Cleaning up in this house. Taking care of all your problems!" She simmered with anger.

"Give me that!" I pulled the plug out of Laura's hand, sat down and started playing. Laura gave up and walked away. Near my electronic piano was a battered paper hang-glider-man toy.

That same night, Toni was under her blankets with the flashlight on. Beneath the covers, Toni drew the Crystal Pegasus based on the drawing that I had given her. Toni had added a man in the moon and five pointed stars in her drawing. The door slammed open, sending a hot square of light across Toni and her bed. She was caught!

The next morning, on a break and alone in my classroom, I was unshaven, with rings under my eyes. I played the piano as harsh sunlight came through the Venetian blinds and painted slashes of light and darkness across the piano and me. Clutching Toni's Crystal Pegasus drawing, Carolyn rushed into the room, slamming the door.

"David, I need to talk with you.... I really appreciate all the time and the attention you've given Toni. I really do," she said.

"She's a great kid. She's bright, creative and she's got a great ear. You know I played some of my CD for her. And she sat right down at the keyboard and picked out the melody. She's truly talented. And what an imagination. We have a great time together."

"That's what I wanted to talk to you about. I'm thrilled she's interested in music, and I've always encouraged her to play. But she's getting a little too carried away with all this. The last few nights I've gotten up and found her awake at the keyboard—with her headphones on—trying to play the music from your CD. Last night, I found her up at four in the morning drawing this."

She handed me Toni's drawing.

"All of a sudden her head is full of this crazy dream—"

"She's a creative child. She can do anything," I said.

"That's right. She's just a child, who doesn't know the difference between the real world and all these dreams. She believes everything you say. She thinks all this magical dream stuff is real."

"The world is magical. I was just trying to expose her to all the possibilities that life has to offer," I said.

"She's six. All she needs to be exposed to is playing t-ball, baking brownies, and slumber parties. A normal happy childhood. A foundation for a normal happy life, filled with things she can count on. A real life. I don't want her to grow with her head full of crazy dreams. Wanting to live some crazy lifestyle, touring on the road. Trading a real life to chase some dream."

"Dreams make a life real," I said.

"Yeah. Well, I was there when the dream turned into the nightmare. Do you even remember? It's me. I was on that Crystal Pegasus tour. I rode the Crystal Pegasus with you— 'til it crashed," Carolyn said.

"Are we talking about Toni or you? I was talking about your daughter," I said.

"I was talking about our daughter," Carolyn said, quietly.

That's when I realized the truth and all the pieces connected.

"I really wanted to tell you, David. I meant to call—" Carolyn said.

My hand crushed the drawing, and I stood up.

"What! Calling me didn't make it into your day planner! It's been six years!"

"I know, seven since you left," Carolyn said.

"I did not leave you. You walked out on me without a word!"

"No, you left. You disappeared into a vial of coke. No, this is not working. I'm going to need to take her out of day camp and—"

"She's my daughter—You can't just play God like this. You took her away. She'll never have—I'll never have those years. You took six years away from—" I said.

"I didn't take them away. You shoved them up your nose." Carolyn slammed the door, and I slid down the wall, where I had been cornered. She had reminded me of how I had let cocaine destroy our life together. I let out an anguished cry and slammed my fist on the floor. I crumpled into a pain-wracked heap.

That afternoon, in our apartment, I grabbed my backpack. Laura tried to talk to me as I ran around the apartment, throwing CDs into the pack's front pouch. The afternoon sun made harsh, crooked pools of light that flashed across Laura and me as we ran back and forth.

"What did the doctor say?" Laura asked.

"I'm pregnant."

"That's not funny," she said.

"I'm going to be late for the session," I said. Out of the corner of my eye, I saw my face reflected on a clock. I was looking thinner and sicklier. I put sheet music I had written into the backpack. I coughed and rubbed my chest and arms.

"Dammit, David! Look at you; you look like hell. This album isn't worth you getting sick."

I moved Laura out of the way. She slapped my hands off her shoulders.

"I gotta go. We'll talk later," I said.

"No, we won't! You never have the time! We gotta talk now!"

She grabbed my arm.

"LATER!" I yelled, wrenching my arm away.

I slammed the door behind me.

"David!" Then sadly Laura said, "David."

Her face hardened with determination. Laura darted to another part of the room.

Walking quickly down the street and lost in my worries, I bumped into some guy. I didn't see his face, but I noticed that he dropped a red rose.

"Open your eyes! I'm walking here!" the man said.

I tore swiftly away.

Soon, I was trudging past the street where Trudy had died. In a hurry, I moved along. Then something caught my eye. "Trudy!" I called out.

I ran to her, spun her around, and she was alive! She smiled warmly.

Trudy stood up out of her wheelchair!

"You're standing!"

"It's a dream, dummy," Trudy said.

Suddenly we were in a different place standing on a bridge. I looked around—surprised by the new location. I hugged Trudy. She held me warmly and patted me on the back.

Trudy smiled and said, "I came back for two reasons. First, you're slow. Second, there's something you need to know—"

Without a warning, I was pulled away from Trudy—until she was only a small figure on the far away bridge... I heard a voice.

"David," Mark said. I woke up and saw that I was at Mark's home. I had been dozing.

"What? Uh—Damn." I felt so disappointed that I hadn't heard Trudy's advice.

"Hey, I've moved the equipment. Let's get back in the studio," Mark said. Still intensely disappointed, I got up and shuffled to Mark's studio room.

Twenty minutes later, I was frustrated, and I slammed down some sheet music.

"Can you speed up the process between takes?" I said.

Mark tossed my Paper-Hang-gliderman and said, "Can you get this—pipe dream—out of my way?"

"I'll hang-glide some day," I said.

"You won't."

"I will!" I insisted.

"Bet!"

"Come on."

"No, I mean it. Bet," Mark repeated.

"I'm not gonna take your money."

"That's true. A hundred dollars."

"Mark. Stop it."

"Chicken."

"Hey!"

"Hundred bucks, come on! Chicken!" Mark made clucking sounds. "One hundred dollars."

"Okay!" I said. "Roll the tape."

Mark started the tape. I made a mistake.

"DAMN," I said.

Mark's eyes went wide. "Easy, man. Maybe, you want a break."

"How many songs have we finished?

"Four."

"How many songs to go?"

"Nine."

"How long does it take to finish a song?"

"Two weeks—give or take."

I did frantic calculating in my mind, and said, "No. No break. Not enough time."

"Enough time for what?" Mark asked.

I did *not* tell him. I could have said, "Only one week for me to be alive! I'll be dead. The album won't be done. And there'll be nothing! No music. No contribution. No meaning. Nothing!" No, I did not tell Mark my fears. I did not share the sobbing that was in my heart.

"Forget it. Roll the tape," I said.

Mark frowned, then pressed the button and engaged the tape deck.

That afternoon, I walked up the stairs of my apartment building. The wind blew furiously. I caught a glimpse of my face reflected on the window of my downstairs neighbor's apartment. Laura was right. The rings under my eyes and the pallor of my face made me look like death's leftovers. I remembered Dr. Stewart's voice, "I don't want to give you false hope; you have two months left, maybe three." That meant I only had a week.

I said to myself, "Not enough time...Gotta tell Laura. Laura will help me."

I staggered up the steps.

I opened the door to the apartment. The wind slammed the door shut behind me. I came upon Laura's "Happy Birthday" sign. The shades were down, and one stripe of light slashed across a note attached to the bottom of the birthday sign. The room was filled with ominous shadows. Near the note, my paper hang-glider toy dangled...

The note read:
> David,
> I tried and I tried. I can't take it, anymore. I'll call you sometime.
> Laura

I grabbed the note and ripped it down off the thumbtack. The ripping sound reverberated in the empty apartment. All the life had left the apartment with Laura's departure. I noticed my therapist, Adina's picture on a newsletter, and I picked up the phone and dialed her number. I heard Adina's answering machine message: "Thank you for calling. For the next week I will be at the International Healers Conference in Paris. If this is an emergency, my colleague Dr. Natalie—"

I slammed the phone down. I pressed the playback button on my answering machine and heard Mark's message: "Uh, David. Hi. Mark. Just to remind you, that Jennifer and I are out of town for the weekend—in Tahoe. Just in case you got the itch for a surprise session. Well, you can't. See you later. Bye."

I fumbled through some papers and read: "Day Camp Registration: Child: Toni Verdoux. Mother: Carolyn Verdoux." And I saw their phone number.

I dialed and Carolyn answered, "Hello?"

"Carolyn, let me speak with Toni," I said.

"David? Toni's asleep. She's taking a nap before dinner. This late night drawing is—I'm afraid she's going to get sick. You shouldn't put crazy—"

I hung up.

Frantically, I looked through my little phone/address book and found the entry: "Laura's Mom—Mrs. Evan Marshall and her phone number. I dialed desperately and heard an answering machine message—"Hello. If this is Maggie, sorry I won't be able to play bridge this week—"

I slammed down the phone. I realized that Laura had run home and probably they used her Mom's favorite solution for a problem—running off on a vacation.

I was seized by a coughing fit, and I staggered to the bathroom. I coughed up blood, which splattered on the mirror over the sink. I saw the reflection of my haggard face through the dripping blood.

Staggering out of the bathroom, I reached for my flute quiver. It was empty.

"My flute! Where?!" I said.

I tore around the apartment frantically looking for my flute. I couldn't find it.

Minutes later, I was at the cemetery, I staggered among the gravestones. A savage wind lashed at my hair. I felt ravaged with pain and felt absolutely alone and lost. The wind threw leaves and dirt into my face. The wind tore my hat off, and I gave chase until I found my hat plastered against a tombstone.

Flashes of memory consumed my senses.

"You didn't have time for me or Toni! Dreams don't make a good father! You didn't have time—" Carolyn said.

"I've been nothing but supportive. There's a limit," Laura said.

"Can I learn to draw that?" Toni asked.

"Dreams don't make a good father," Carolyn said.

"There's a limit," Laura said.

"Can I learn—"

"Dreams don't make a good father—" Carolyn said.

"There's a limit," Laura said.

"Can I—" Toni said.

"There's a limit. There's a limit. There's a limit," Laura said.

I felt a tornado of emotion ripping through my chest. My thoughts whirled. "I can't finish the album! I can't! I can't! Laura don't leave me...don't leave..."

I screamed and sobbed. Between the gravestones, I lay face down, fiercely shutting my eyes.

I was a small figure in the middle of the maelstrom of wind, leaves, and dust.

An hour later I climbed, like an old man, up the steps of my apartment building in darkness. I opened the door and saw the apartment still empty and lifeless.

In the restroom, I turned on the bathtub water facet.

Water flowed, filling the tub. The blood still remained on the mirror.

Slowly, I settled in the water until only my eyes were visible.

I found myself in my day camp classroom. It was nighttime. I felt disorientated. A moment later, I took a sheet of paper, folded it into a handmade card, and wrote a note that ended with "please forgive me…"

I closed the card and wrote Laura on it.

I looked up and saw both Laura and Carolyn standing tall and above me. I handed the note to Laura but the note burst into flame.

Laura turned away from me—eerily—almost mechanically.

I finished another homemade card asking for forgiveness and wrote "Carolyn" on its cover. I handed the note to Carolyn and— it burst into flame.

Carolyn turned away. I reached my hand toward the women while anguish wracked my body. The women ignored me. I couldn't breathe.

I woke up in the bathtub, coughing up water. My body felt like lead and I barely got out of the tub. My feet left water footprints on the bathroom floor.

I coughed again, tasted metal and salt, and rubbed my mouth. I left a bloody handprint on the door. Stepping out of the bathroom, I remembered Dr. Stewart's voice saying, "David, if you cough up blood, have Laura take you to the hospital immediately. You could be near death."

Sweat dripped from my forehead, stinging my eyes. I collapsed into the bed, and brought the covers up.

A white flash—

I was hit by the Intruder, and was thrown to the ground. I put my hands up and kicked and punched toward the Intruder. Again and again the Intruder struck me and knocked me to the ground. I was hurt badly and exhausted. I heard Adina's voice saying: "What you resist, persists,"

"Trust," Laura's voice said.

I shook my head, and ignored their advice. I just kept kicking. The Intruder struck again, slamming me to the ground. I saw Toni poking her head up from behind a ridge. She winced with each blow that landed on me. Weakened, I could not get up. My face was a swollen mess. I tasted metal and salt.

The Intruder stepped away from me and its shadow fell across Toni. Panic washed over her, and she stood frozen. The Intruder grabbed her hand, pulling her towards a cliff.

"No!" I yelled.

Dangling by the Intruder's grip, Toni screamed as she looked down. Her right shoe fell off her foot and plummeted to the rocks below.

Terror rose up in my throat. I must save my daughter. But my body was a battered mess. I tried to get up. I couldn't. I tried again and again. Finally, my muscles and gut screaming in agony, I made it to my feet. Somehow I dislodged the Intruder's grip on my daughter.

I pulled Toni back from the edge. She was all right. Then, the Intruder's claw grabbed the back of my shirt and threw me into a wheelchair!

Straps slammed on my wrists—I was trapped. The Intruder pushed me. The wheelchair and I plummeted over the cliff edge. I fell and fell ... Toni screamed ... then nothing but darkness.

Chapter Eight

Startled, I awoke in bed. My sweat made the sheets cling to me. I blinked. Sweat stung my eyes. I was near death. And back in my nightmare—

Darkness. Then ... a fluttering of light. The edge of a sheet flapped, giving me a partial view of something outside the sheet. I could barely see the wheelchair on its side, one wheel spinning. I was face down in the sand, having fallen several feet. Only through my left eye, I saw my situation. Covered by this sheet, a morgue sheet?, I felt my face, my body all in great pain. It means I'm still alive. *But I know I'm on the edge to go either way—to death or stay here in this excruciating pain?*

The sheet fluttered. Toni now held my hand. Her tears fell.

No, Toni, I won't leave you. Not now. Not that we're together.

I tried to rise. The sheet held me down. Somehow the sheet was smothering me. Some form of supernatural weight on me.

No! I will not go quietly.

Something in my pocket.

Toni's eyes went wide. I used my Swiss army knife to cut through the sheet.

The tear in the sheet got larger and larger, until, triumphantly, I emerged, reborn—stronger. Light emanated from my body. I stood tall.

Toni jumped into my arms. We embraced.

I took in a deep breath and took a glance at the ocean. I thought I'd never see it again after my fall off the cliff.

That's when I saw the Intruder. About twenty feet away. It stood there. Waiting.

I put Toni down, and gave her a reassuring squeeze on her shoulder.

I took a breath, pulled back my shoulders and marched toward the Intruder.

I clenched my fists, placing them in a fighting posture.

The Intruder sent a fire-beam of energy. I fell; my legs were left as burning stumps—mid-thigh (just like the Intruder's attack before). On the ground, I saw a Ring of Fire form around me. In the fire, I saw a series of images:

- I used a straw to inhale cocaine.

- I was with party girls who also did drugs.

- An old photo of Carolyn and me as a happy couple burned.

- A newspaper clipping: "David Nouveau Wows Fans on his 'Crystal Pegasus Tour'" burned.

- I opened the letter that read "Divorce."

- Carolyn yelled at me.

- Laura yelled at me.

But somehow, I sensed a presence. I turned my head, looking away from the Ring of Fire.

I saw Trudy, standing about ten feet away from me.

Trudy said, "Look somewhere else."

I looked skyward, feeling a Source of energy. Then I looked down and saw water was in my hands…

The water put out the fire of the photograph of Carolyn with me and extinguished the newspaper clipping. The water still flowed from my hands. And superimposed in the water were images of joy:

- I helped Mark, listening to him amid his recording equipment.

- I told the Crystal Pegasus story, and saw the happy faces of my day camp children.

- Bathed in love and light, Laura and I danced and kissed.

- and I bounced Toni on my knee with her giggles of "Bounce me higher!"

Suddenly, I found myself waist-deep in a lake. Where there had been flames, was now sparkling water. I caught my breath as I glimpsed a reflection of Crystal Pegasus flow over the water. The lake hid my damaged legs.

Trudy stood on the ground near the lake's edge. She said, "Step up, David. Step up."

I stepped up onto the bank—and my legs were healed and whole!

Trudy hugged me. Then she stepped back. There was a stairway. Across the steps above me was the large shadow of The Intruder. I walked up the stairs to a plateau where the Intruder stood. I instinctively clenched my fists. In my mind, I heard Adina's voice: "What you resist, persists."

I opened my fists. The Intruder rushed toward me, and I used the Aikido Move I had learned from Adina. Again and again, the Intruder lunged at me and I answered with the Aikido Move, slamming the Intruder down.

I threw the Intruder off the plateau; it crashed down upon the morgue sheet I had escaped. The morgue sheet wrapped itself around the Intruder like a Venus flytrap. The sheet constricted. I could see the Intruder's claws trying to poke through the sheet, but *it could not release itself. As the sheet constricted smaller, I could hear the Intruder's bones breaking—and an unearthly screeching. The sheet constricted until it was the size of a shoebox. Then it changed form until it was a red rose. I picked up the rose....*

With a gasp, I awoke breathing heavily in my bed. As I caught my breath, I grabbed a pillow and rubbed the sweat from my face.

I felt sore, really sore. But I knew, I knew it in my gut that my fever had broken.

I saw a red rose on the floor. I was stunned. Still I picked up the rose.

While I placed the rose into a small vase, about one mile away, Jennifer drove up to the cemetery entrance which was framed by two rose bushes. She got out of the car and looked over at Mark who stepped from the passenger seat.

Mark and Jennifer walked down a hill at the cemetery. He looked into her eyes, and she nodded. She waited as Mark continued walking.

With the shades drawn, it was dark in my apartment. I lit a candle. The flickering flame created a magical atmosphere.

I grabbed a sheet of paper and folded it into a homemade greeting card. I wrote *Laura* on the outside (just as I had done in my recent nightmare). I opened my card and wrote "Laura, my love."

At the cemetery, Mark kneeled before Debbie's gravestone. He then pulled a jewelry box out of his pocket. He removed the pin from his collar. With reverence, he held the pin, the gift from his deceased wife. Then he placed it in the box.

Mark kissed his hand and gently, lovingly touched his hand on Debbie's gravestone. Shaking, he finally stood up and then returned to Jennifer. They walked away, hand in hand.

In my apartment, the candle flickered as I wrote "Carolyn" on another handmade card. Soon, with tears in my eyes, I completed the letter to Carolyn. I included the words "then I went into rehabilitation" and finally "Please forgive me." I signed it: "David." Minutes later, I carved Toni's name on a candle.

While I was carving my daughter Toni's name on a candle, about ten blocks away, her mother Carolyn was towering over little Toni. They confronted each other in their living room.

"Now, Toni, you don't—" Carolyn said.

"No, you're not listening. David listens to me and—"

"I don't want to hear it! I'm your mother and—!" Carolyn said.

In my apartment, I felt moved to continue my impromptu ritual. I lit Toni's candle. I placed a candle inscribed "Music" near other candles with the carved names of Carolyn and Laura. There was a knock at the door. I looked up.

"Laura?" I said.

I opened the door.

"Toni!" I said upon seeing my little girl.

"Hi, David," Toni said. Evidently Carolyn had not told Toni that I was her father. I felt my heart sink upon not hearing her say the word: "Dad."

"Come in. Does your mother know?"

"No!" she said, and ran through the doorway and up the

stairs.

I dialed Carolyn's number, and she answered immediately. I let her know that Toni was safe, and Carolyn agreed when I suggested that I walk Toni to their home. After hanging up, I asked Toni how she knew where I lived.

She said simply, "Mom and I were driving past one day. And you went into this building. So I thought it was probably your home."

"Oh, you're a detective, too—huh?"

Toni smiled at that. Then, I did a magic trick of pulling a "light ball of energy" out of thin air...

"Wow! Cool!" Toni said.

Minutes later, Toni and I walked at the nearby park. My heart twinged because this was the same park where Laura and I had crossed toy swords in playful battles.

"Do I have to go home now?" Toni asked.

"I don't want your mother worrying about you." I said.

"All right," she said.

"David, you didn't finish telling the Crystal Pegasus story," Toni said.

"Oh, yeah. Now, let's see—"

"Crystal Pegasus was on the cliff," Toni said.

I jumped up on a garbage can, and I said, "Crystal Pegasus was up there. And he's trying to get up his courage...He's scared...But he wants to fly. He pauses...He listens...And he hears an idea in his mind: You gotta live Your Dreams!"

As I said this—I could hear Trudy's voice in my mind saying, "You've gotta live your dreams."

A decision on my face, I tipped over like I was going to dive toward water. I jumped—and landed on the ground and mimed flying!

"And he flaps and flaps and he's flying! He soars into the sky—and he picks up someone special!" I picked up Toni. A moment later, after I put her down, she showed me some karate moves. Strange. Karate was part of Toni's childhood—just like it had been part of mine. We did the moves together. Then, she danced and cart wheeled along, and I energetically matched her movements...until she did the "splits"—with her legs stretched flat on the ground.

"You're kidding," I said.

A moment later, we walked hand-in-hand.

"David?" Toni said.

"Toni?" I said, playfully.

"David?"

"Toni?!"

"No. I'm serious."

"Okay," I said.

"Will you be my Daddy?"

My face trembled.

"Yes," I said, and I opened my arms. And Toni rushed into my arms, and we hugged.

Fifteen minutes later, I watched as Toni closed the door to her home behind her. I stood there a moment. Then, I reached into my pocket and pulled out an envelope addressed to Carolyn. My hand shook as I put the envelope into Carolyn's mailbox.

When I returned to the empty apartment, I started playing the piano. And for the first time in days, the music flowed easily. I was feeling better, more alive. I started ad-libbing lyrics to a song I made up for the first time.

"See

The light..."

I played a few notes and continued singing:

"See
The light
In the night
And I'll be there."

I felt myself flow with the song, and everything else faded away. I felt elated and connected with the music.

The next day, after my classes, I played the piano in my day camp classroom. While I played, Carolyn quieted entered, holding my letter. I looked up. Not knowing what to say, I just stopped playing.

"That's nice. Don't stop. Please," she said.

"I'm glad you're here," I said.

"This was some letter. I didn't know. When did you go in?" Carolyn asked.

"Six months after you left."

"How long were you in rehab?" she said referring to my participating in a rehabilitation program to wean myself off cocaine.

"Technically, four months in residence. Six months daily group and other things. But it's a life-long process," I said.

She nodded.

"You know, I met you about a year or so after my mom died," Carolyn said.

"I remember," I said.

"I never told you but...she died of alcoholism."

"Your mom—But she was so beautiful in those photos," I said.

"She was a binge drinker. My dad loved her so much, but he didn't know what to do. When she was dying, I felt so helpless. I couldn't save her. Then we met; it was so magical. I thought all that bad stuff was behind me. When we went on tour, I realized I couldn't save you. But when I found out about the baby, I realized I could save *her*."

I reached for Carolyn's hand. She squeezed my hand in return. In that instant, the connection was back. It was like a moment out of our first year together.

"Our daughter has a lot of you in her," she said.

"Oh, lucky you!"

"Yes," Carolyn said sincerely.

"Any requests?" I asked.

"How about that one—you know, 'I wouldn't have missed it.'"

"Yes," I said.

I played the song. We both smiled, finally at ease with each other.

Minutes later, Carolyn and I were dancing in my day camp classroom.

Laura arrived at the door and saw Carolyn in my arms. Carolyn's eyes went wide, fearing Laura's jealousy.

Chapter Nine

Laura hesitated, looking at Carolyn in my arms as we finished a dance move. I could see it on Carolyn's face; she was waiting for Laura to scream at us. A moment passed, and I gently waved Laura over to us.

In my mind I saw images of my dancing with both women.

I held the hand of each, simultaneously sending them both spinning outward. Carolyn dropped out after a bit.

My momentary reverie ended, and in reality I was gliding with Laura. We were an obvious match. A bit of regret, a touch of envy, momentarily flashed in Carolyn's eyes. But she smiled wistfully. Laura and I stopped in a pose. Carolyn applauded for us. She noticed her watch, and said, "Wow, two hours went fast. I better get home. My sister and Toni will be getting back from a movie."

Carolyn joined me and Laura near the door. I held my hand out to Carolyn.

"Well, take care of yourself," I said.

Carolyn and I held each other's hand, then we both moved and gave each other a hug.

"Tell Toni, I miss her."

"I will," she said.

I watched Carolyn leave. Then, I turned to Laura. And her look nearly froze me on the spot.

"You all right?" I asked.

"No! Don't you treat me like an afterthought! I come back, and you don't even.... You're going to have to do better than this!" Laura quickly darted out of the room. I followed.

"Laura!"

She ran down the steps. I ran after her, but I heard the door slam.

At the bottom of the stairs, I opened the door and looked both ways. Laura was gone!

On the street, I ran, looking for Laura. I couldn't find her. I had lost her again.

I went to our apartment, but it was still empty. I felt my stomach heave, and I almost threw up. I put a couple of things into my waist-pack and ran out the door. I ran to the park where we had shared the fun times with the toy swords and even dancing on the boat in the playground. Laura was nowhere to be found. I felt my heart twisted in pain. But I would not stop. I would find Laura!

I climbed over the fence of the backyard belonging to Laura's mother. I decided not to go through the front of the building because it would be too easy for Laura's mother to act as the gatekeeper to keep me away from Laura.

In the backyard, I looked up and saw Laura at the top of the staircase—five stories up. This was the place she had told me was her favorite retreat when she was a little girl. Laura had tried to share the view with me, but my fear of heights had kept us apart. I put my foot on the staircase—it squeaked. I looked up and Laura was still reading her book up there. I put my foot on another stair, and it squeaked also. Now, I had a new idea, but I shook with terror. I climbed up the side of the staircase like it was a scaffold.

At the fourth level, I slipped! I barely caught myself on the third level. I looked down, and was afraid but I kept on climbing. At the top, Laura did not notice that I was climbing up the side of the staircase. Moments later, through a hole between slats of the banister, a white flag rose up. The flag waved in surrender. Laura saw that!

Then through the same space between the slats, a red rose appeared with a note attached. Laura's face softened. I climbed onto the top level.

"I didn't hear you walk up," Laura said.

Laura saw my expression.

"No, you didn't climb—" And she looked over the edge. It was a real high view. I nodded. She knew what kind of effort I had expended to surprise her. I had slain the dragon of my fear of heights—for her. And she knew it.

She waved me toward her, saying, "Come here, my spider dude."

We came together in a heartfelt embrace.

"I'm out of remission." I finally said it. Admitting it to her. Admitting it to myself.

Laura held me tighter.

"We'll get through this; we always do," Laura said.

And I knew somehow we would.

Chapter Ten

Three years later, the sun made the flowers of our backyard glow. Nearby, the Crystal Pegasus figurine had riders, Laura and me as a cutout couple in wedding attire.

I held Laura's hand and placed the ring on her finger. And I was sitting in a wheelchair. My illness had resurfaced enough to make me so weak that I could not walk. But I was still in the game. I was working with another cancer specialist, having given Dr. Stewart the boot! I continued working with Adina.

I had enjoyed three years of health and vigor. Three years longer than Dr. Stewart's prediction. Although, I was in the wheelchair—I was getting married to my soul mate! In that moment, I was feeling grace just like Adina had mentioned. I nodded at Adina, and she smiled in return.

I had dreaded a return to the wheelchair. But that afternoon, with Laura's hand in mine and wedding rings on our fingers, the situation felt so different. I even found a way to dance with Laura. With her dancing in front of me, I rocked my wheelchair. Left wheel forward then right wheel forward. Then I spun my wheelchair around. Trudy would have been proud of me. I was thinking of her—so she was present in a way. "Live your dreams," Trudy had said. And I was doing just that. In my deepest heart, I dreamed of closeness and love. And I had that with Laura. Also, Adina was right—even in the wheelchair, I could still feel FREE. I could move, I could dance. A bit limited, but I could move. My heart could move—as Laura hugged me and kissed me.

Nearby, Carolyn stood with Toni at this wedding. Three years had given Toni plenty of time to grow taller. I rolled up to her, and Toni gave me a hug.

"Happy Wedding Day, Daddy," Toni said. I smiled and nodded to Carolyn. I was so grateful about the peace between us, making an oasis for my daughter.

Later, Laura was on my lap and she was pleasantly rubbing her tummy with our little baby on the way. Jennifer and Mark were still together, and they were belly dancing. Our other friends held hands and danced in a circle around Laura and me. She gave me a sweet kiss.

* * *

The next day, I was at the edge of a cliff. I looked down with trepidation—just like Crystal Pegasus in my story. I took a deep breath, preparing myself. In my mind's eye, I could see Trudy's smiling face. She had told me, "You've gotta live your dreams."

"Okay, Trudy, I'm gonna step up," I thought.

I threw on my safety helmet. Mark stood next to me as I shifted in my wheelchair. He handed me a $100 bill, fulfilling our bet. Smiling in triumph, I put the $100 into a pocket that I zipper-closed.

Laura kissed me. She and Mark helped me out of my

wheelchair and into a hang-glider harness.

Using the hang-glider, I soared off the cliff. My heart was beating so fast—I was excited, I was terrified. I was thrilled to be alive. As I banked the hang-glider, I caught a glimpse of my Crystal Pegasus Image that was a logo on the wing of my hang-glider.

I am Crystal Pegasus, and I can fly!

Afterward to *Living*

I'm grateful to my editor Barry Adamson II for his work on this current version of the *Living* story. Thank you Johanna Ellen Mac Leod for your comments and insights.

Living began as a screenplay that helped me launch a career in the US film industry. The then-California Motion Picture Commissioner was impressed with my work. This gave me a big opportunity to have two unique resources when I directed my first feature film: the California Motion Picture Commissioner set up the San Luis Obispo Airport and an American Eagle airplane for free—for use in that production.

Living was also the first time I expressed the Crystal Pegasus story—now a graphic novel available on Amazon.com.

For this reason, I have many people to thank for previous versions of *Living*—both in audio and filmed formats.

Thank you to:

Randi Acton, Barry Adamson II, David MacDowell Blue, Daniel Buhlman, Linda L. Chappo, Joanne Chew, Libba Cooperman, JoAnn Dahlkoetter, Justin H., K.H., Alexis

Hernandez, Michael Hicks, Jeff Hixon, Stacy Diane Horn, Jaymie Lam, Hollie Lamarr, Paula Landers, PML, Johanna Ellen Mac Leod, Thelma M., Richard San Martin, Sari Jozokos Morninghawk, Colin Nasseri, K. Nguyen, Norman Pascoe, Shayna Pascoe, Jacquie Schmall, Stephanie Serra, Karen Thomas, Dave Thude, Richard Vitale, Maryann Wagner, Carol Wilkinson, Bill Williams, Dan Wilson.

Our apologies for not having access to a few names at press time. We are still grateful.

Jenalee Storm: Storm Warning

A Short Story by Tom Marcoux
Based on a premise by Tom Marcoux and
Johanna Ellen Mac Leod

He was gorgeous. And he knew I had just broken up with my boyfriend of two years.

Sure, he was all sweet and he listened. And he didn't rush me. Did I say he was gorgeous?

And he was scum. That's right. Joseph Hayden Grantsen was and is a prick.

I found this out yesterday by glancing at Joseph's wall on Facebook. He was flirting with two chicks. When I confronted him about whether he was sleeping with either, I saw it on his face. He WAS cheating on me!

I felt like casting a spell to melt him from his dick to his toenails.

But I didn't. *The Wiccan Rede* holds the principle: "An Ye Harm None."

"Couldn't I give him a hangnail at least?"

"No way," said my best friend, Satrenda.

The first year of college. A new town for me, and I knew no one. Until I met Satrenda.

"Jenalee Storm. That's a good name," she said, her bright smile lit up her chocolate-tinted face.

"Really?"

"Sure. It's three syllables and then 'bam.' It's music," Satrenda confirmed.

"What kind of name is Satrenda?" I asked her when we first met.

"It's the kind when parents think they're clever. And they're not," she said.

Satrenda and I had met when we were standing in line to get our classes adjusted.

Hmmm. I guess she's right about my name. She'd know. She's a music major.

My major? I don't know. Not yet. Give me a break. I'm seventeen; I graduated high school early. I do my best to live up to "young woman." I don't like the label "girl."

Later that day, I walked to the campus bookstore. Coming around a corner, I tripped over a ridge in the cement. I dropped my books. This guy stepped over, reaching to help me with the books. He said, "You want some help with—?"

"No, I—" I saw his face. Perfect. A sparkle in his blue eyes, warm smile. He made Joseph Hayden Grantsen look like a Denebian slime devil. Okay, that's probably my last reference to something from *Star Trek*. Maybe.

I was going to say to the guy I didn't need help, but I'm not stupid. I let him help me. Heck, I'd let him kiss me. That didn't happen.

"I'm Daniel," he said.

"I'm Jenalee," I managed to say.

He took my hand. Oooh. Tingles. This is something

special.

I know about these things. Since that time I said to my grandmother, "Gram-Gram, I saw the pokadice."

"Poka—what?" Gram-Gram asked.

My six-year-old mouth couldn't say the word. "You know. Floating person."

"You mean poltergeist," Gram-Gram said.

"Yeah. Polta—porah. What you said," I replied.

You see "poltergeist" is German for "noisy ghost."

Back to Daniel—blue eyes—be still my heart . . . Yeah, him.

"You're taking psychology?" Daniel asked, eyeing my General Psychology textbook.

"Yeah."

"Maybe we'll be in the same class," Daniel said. His cell phone chimed.

"Oh, it's my Dad. See you around, right?" He stepped away.

For sure! I thought.

"Earth to Jenalee," Satrenda said, when she arrived at my side.

* * *

One month later, I'm standing on a mansion's right side balcony seven stories up. About ten feet away, Daniel is unconscious on the roof top that stands between two balconies about thirty feet apart. At the other side, my opponent, Sable Cane, stands. She's tall with model features to match, and like a starving model, she's furious. She's killed four people including her own father. By the way, that was Daniel's father, too.

I hate this bitch.

I've learned much about the Craft, summoning the energies of nature. My grandmother taught me how to do things for healing and for good.

Now, I've got to defend myself from things I never faced before.

A storm rages.

A lightning bolt strikes the balcony.

"Shit!"

It almost took off my arm, but instead, it disintegrated a whole section of the banister.

How's Sable doing that?

That's nothing that I've been taught.

"So Jenalee, you care about Daniel?" Sable calls out.

I say nothing. I'll use my words to distract her later.

"What good does your Wicca help you now, Jenalee? You don't know the power bestowed by Drenbahk," Sable says, referring to the demon she had welcomed.

Sable raises her right hand and directs lightning to strike near me again. The house shakes. Daniel's left leg slides. Any second he'll slide right off the roof!

"There is something I know," I say under my breath. I reach to the bolas, used like a belt around my waist.

I throw my bolas which whip through the air. The heavy weights on the end of three strands ensnare Sable's right arm, pining it to the nearby banister.

"Hematite grounds energy," I say, referring to the hematite I had placed into my bolas as weights.

Deprived of her magic, Sable reaches into her handbag and pulls a knife.

She'll be free in a moment.

A moment might prove enough for me to . . .

* * *

Afterward to *Jenalee Storm*

The above is a preview of Jenalee Storm. I'm grateful for my training as an actor. It helps me get into "the voice" of Jenalee. Thanks to Johanna Ellen Mac Leod. She and I expect that Jenalee will be seen next in a series of novels or graphic novels.

Jenalee and her team, including Satrenda and Daniel, face supernatural opponents, concurrently with Jenalee's college adventures. She studies abroad in Venice, Italy and other places–as she continues her quest to protect the innocent from dark evils.

Tom Marcoux

Jack AngelSword

I swung my AngelSword, and my brother Sal blocked it and renewed his attack.

My brother wanted to kill me. These last 24 hours brought me news: I had a brother. He's a homicidal maniac. By the way, he stole my goddaughter's dredaya which she needs to stay alive.

So he wants to kill a six year old girl.

I swung my AngelSword and struck Sal's leg!

My sword rebounded amid a shower of sparks.

What?

"Jack, this is not your day," Sal said, tearing away the tattered remnant of his trousers over his left leg.

I saw a cyborg-limb replacing his flesh—a second before his metal foot kicked me in the gut.

Fireworks exploded in front of my eyes before I tumbled down a hill, deeper into the cavern.

I didn't have time to admire the shrine to my left, except to note that the Synton Scepter was displayed on a glowing pedestal.

I needed that Synton Scepter as part of my efforts to save my goddaughter's life. Little Cydney would not live to see her 7th birthday if I didn't defeat Sal.

Sal leapt and landed near me. Still flat on the ground, I reached toward the magical sword tattoo on my left arm. In an instant, the AngelSword disappeared from my arm and manifested in my hand.

I barely managed to get to my feet as I ducked Sal's next strike and then swung my AngelSword at Sal.

Our two swords crashed and rang with the impact.

He had some definite advantages over me. Twice as muscular, amazingly quick and with longer arms to match his greater height.

Sal swung. I blocked, and he battered my ribs with another kick. *Can't breathe.* Intense pain.

He slammed the hilt of his sword across my face and kicked me repeatedly.

On the floor, I caught a view of both my half-sister Nia and my love Denise manacled to the cave wall.

"At least give me some sport, brother," Sal said, derision dripping on his words.

"I'm new to this, Sal. Just... just a moment," I said.

He laughed. The cave twisted the sound so it seemed to come from everywhere. I blinked my eyes, my vision blurry.

I feinted toward Sal, then rolled next to Nia.

Holding the AngelSword in my right hand, I slapped Nia's shoulder.

"Nia, wake up!"

Nia returned to consciousness.

"Do something!" I said.

Out of the corner of my eye, I saw Denise drawing her right foot up toward her right manacled hand.

Nia blinked her eyes. Her right hand glowed and a tendril

of energy moved from her hand to my AngelSword. Now both glowed and surged as she extended her will.

A thundering sound—a shockwave of magic extended from the AngelSword and Nia, causing Sal to collapse. The shockwave also knocked Sal's nine soldiers down as they arrived to come to their master's defense. All were temporarily stunned.

Denise finished freeing herself with some form of tool she pulled from her boot.

The manacles around Nia's wrists glowed and dissolved into harmless powder.

After backtracking to where Noah had fallen, Denise and I each grabbed an arm and carried my best friend out of the cave...

* * *

Soon, my assembled "family" scrambled aboard Mrs. Chi's aircraft. Picture the Titanic with two big tubes sticking out of its sides. In essence, it was a small city floating on the winds.

Her long hair billowing like a cape, Nia remained with Noah in the infirmary. Though she'd deny it, she seemed to have developed a bit of affection for my quirky best friend.

Denise and I headed straight to the Deck 1012.

Tanaka (my sword mentor) and Mrs. Chi were in deep conversation. Mrs. Chi's eyebrows raised as she contained her concern about how beaten I looked.

Tanaka turned to me and said simply: "Speak."

"Tanaka-san," I said. "Sal is too strong. Somehow stronger than a human being. Even beyond having a cyborg leg. I don't think I can beat him."

"It is not about beating him," Tanaka said.

"Then I'll die when I face him."

"Then you die."

"Well—damn! That's not what I signed up for. And what good does that do? It won't help me get the dredaya and save Sydney's life."

With a serene but concerned expression, Tanaka said:

"It is about being present in the moment. The superior warrior does not worry about winning or losing. The superior warrior does not worry. Worry is jumping into the future."

He grabbed an apple and tossed it at me.

I missed. I was shocked. My injuries evidently threw off my timing.

Tanaka grabbed a lamp and tossed it at me.

I ducked that.

Smash. The pieces of glass spread over the carpet.

He grabbed a folding chair, collapsed it and tossed it at me.

In an instant, the AngelSword appeared in my hand and I cut the chair in half.

"What were you thinking as you cut the chair?" Tanaka asked.

"... nothing."

"End of lesson," Tanaka said.

* * *

Minutes later, the Captain's voice boomed on the loud speakers: "Mrs. Chi, we're under attack. Two platoons of attackers have boarded the vessel."

"How?" Denise asked.

Tanaka and Mrs. Chi left to defend the bridge.

Mrs. Chi called on a communication device I wore on my

lapel. "Enemy troops are on Level 8."

"Got it," I replied. Denise pulled her twin pistols from her belt. She and I dashed from the room.

I could sense that I was soon going to confront Sal again.

"Stay in the present moment," Tanaka had said.

Would I retain this lesson?

I would find out.

Afterward to *Jack AngelSword*

The above is a preview of *Jack AngelSword*. Some of the best twists and turns await in the graphics novel-trilogy that my team is working on now. People have asked me, "Tom's what's your life work?" I reply, "Definitely, *Jack AngelSword*. It is one of the most important parts of the work I have done as a writer and artist. My goal is that this franchise continues far beyond my lifespan and becomes my legacy."

Jack and his team, including his half-sister, Nia (wielding her magic) travel around the world gathering artifacts from Venice, Italy; Japan; Mayan Ruins in Mexico and more. Jack and his team struggle to keep the forces of evil from using these powerful, diabolical artifacts, which are set to plunge the world into chaotic darkness.

Secrets for Your Own Creative Projects

"What else do you got?" is a frequent question tossed to screenwriters in Hollywood. The screenwriter comes in to pitch an action movie screenplay. But the producer already has three such scripts in development. So she says, "What else do you got?"

One of my goals with this book is to share a number of projects that I have because I'm always preparing to present material to potential investors and other movers and shakers.

To be helpful to you, I'll now share some material that I first presented in my book *Darkest Secrets of Making a Pitch to the Film and Television Industry.*

SECRET #1: "NEEDINESS" GIVES OFF A SMELL —AND IT STINKS

You want to see your screenplay produced, or to get a movie deal. Maybe have a private investor pledge funds to help produce your film. Wanting is good.

It starts the wheels turning, plans shaping, opportunities being created. On the other hand, desperately needing something can torpedo all your efforts. Sounds like a contradiction, doesn't it? But no—the difference between positive ambition and need can be subtle, but in pitching the effect ends up profound.

Positive ambition comes from a sense of purpose, an emotional place of self–confidence and with an enthusiasm you invite others to share. Neediness is an invitation to pity. It hints of fear, timidity, and a lack of will. Positive ambition inspires confidence. Neediness invokes contempt.

Why? People flinch around neediness. It bothers them. Maybe it reminds them too much of a time when they felt weak. Or perhaps they've had bad experiences in the past with those who manipulate through guilt. Many of us have. And they subconsciously feel that if you're desperate, maybe lots of others have seen through you and rejected you already.

You may, in fact, need to sell a screenplay to pay this month's rent. But the point is that you must avoid coming across as needy.

Many years ago, I had a friend who was running a conference. He knew that I had just started as a professional speaker and I wanted to address his conference audience. He rejected my application.

My friend wanted only "established speakers who already had a following." It hurt. And I lost a lot of energy to feeling betrayed, which slowed me down.

Eventually, I took responsibility for my own thoughts and told myself: "This was one possibility. I'll look for many opportunities. I have something valuable to offer and the universe is a large place with many opportunities."

I share this story to illustrate that our thought patterns have power. A strong way to avoid coming across as needy is look on each meeting as one of many opportunities. On the other hand, anyone who looks on one particular meeting as a "one and only opportunity" will feel stressed out.

Along those lines, I invite you to look on each pitching opportunity as an "opportunity to practice." Tell yourself "I'll have many opportunities" — then you can relax a bit.

You can develop your own "many opportunities." Here's how a screenwriter can drop neediness. It's best to have three screenplays:

1. One screenplay that you're marketing.
2. One screenplay that you're finishing.
3. One screenplay that you're starting.

Why? So you won't be devastated if studio executives reject your finished screenplay. Secondly, studio executives often say, "What else have you got?" And you'll have two other projects to bring to their attention.

Having at least three screenplays does wonders for your own well being. You feel stronger. Producer Linda Obst (*Contact* starring Jodie Foster and Matthew McConaughey and *Sleepless in Seattle* starring Tom Hanks and Meg Ryan) told me, "Have multiple projects. When one isn't [getting traction], toss it on the roof." Her "on the roof" comment was about keeping projects to the side, at the ready.

Having multiple projects gives you confidence and you can avoid the appearance of neediness.

Use "want power" and let go of neediness. By this I mean, "You want the person to say 'yes' to your project. But you do not need that particular person or that particular project to go forward. You have other options!"

Neediness is another word for desperation. Desperation is not attractive! What seems like desperation? Asking for validation with questions like: "So you like this project, right?" or "So this is what you're looking for, huh?" Also, desperate people's anguish is expressed with body language like: smiling too much, wringing hands, or leaning too far forward, hoping for the other person to "toss them a bone."

Your countermeasure to appearing needy is to build up your center of strength. You do that by focusing on empowering thoughts. Here are four elements:

1. Focus on the value you bring

Let's face it: There is no movie without a screenplay. A great film usually begins with a great screenplay. So if you're a screenwriter, you're bringing value (because, of course, you've written a good script!).

As a producer, you bring value when offering a film investment opportunity. The investor's money may just sit in some account. But when the investor has the opportunity to invest in your film, she is helping bring something good into the world. You even give her something to talk about at parties.

2. You are meeting the other person as a peer

Sure, the other person may have higher social status or more money, but you share the same value as a fellow human being. And, according to pitch-master Oren Klaff, you can emphasize your *"situational status."* Your expertise and the unique details of your project is why everyone has gathered to hear your pitch. That's the basis of your situational status. Be sure to focus on the empowered attitude that you are "sharing something valuable" with the people assembled. That's when you become a peer. Everyone in the room puts something valuable on the table. Remember, you are the catalyst. When you pitch, you bring something new and valuable into the room.

3. You have the confidence that you're going to meet several people and you're offering the opportunity to do something exciting and profitable

It's an opportunity to be in business with you. Why? Because you have done your homework and have something valuable to offer. Whether you pitch to a studio executive, a name actor, a producer or a private investor, you already have a plan to meet a number of people. Why is that important? Because no one person holds your fate in his or her hands. You're going to talk to several people and then you ultimately pick who you'll work with—among those who express interest.

I tell myself before a meeting, "Let's find out who wants to play." After you find interested parties, think about who may be a match. Some people really would be a bad match with your offering. Meet them and move on to better prospects.

4. Keep your faith that the right people and right elements will fall into place

When you study case histories, you discover that projects met setback after setback after setback. Yet, the right people ultimately came together. Big projects or small, business or art or educational, engineering or sports—it happens. Time and again.

Producer Brian Grazer brought his film project, a romantic comedy about a man, a mermaid and modern–day Manhattan to the studios for eight years. And personnel at all the studios rejected the project. By the time he returned to Disney, the company was starting up a new division, Touchstone Pictures, and then—and only then—did *Splash* find a home as the first feature film released by Touchstone Pictures!

Keep your faith. Realize that things keep changing, new trends start becoming popular, friends get new jobs, and rivals move away or fade away.

Getting things done requires time and persistence. For example, David Webb Peoples wrote a screenplay, *The William Munny Killings*, in 1976. Clint Eastwood purchased it in 1979 but waited until 1991 to film the screenplay as *Unforgiven*. The film won four Oscars: Best Picture, Best Director (Clint Eastwood), Best Supporting Actor (Gene Hackman) and Best Editing (Joel Cox). It was nominated for five other awards, including Eastwood as Best Actor. Peoples won L.A. Film Critics and National Society of Film Critics awards for best screenplay.

During the long wait before *Unforgiven* came to fruition, Peoples wrote numerous other screenplays—many were produced and he even directed a feature film based on one.

Keep your faith—and that requires self–discipline. You must focus on empowered thoughts. Some people like to focus on affirmations—statements that are personal, present tense and positive. Here's an affirmation: "I am selling a screenplay today." Some people report affirmations help a lot. Other people say, "Affirmations don't work for me because part of me feels that I'm lying to myself."

Instead, I prefer asking empowering questions and providing myself with answers. This process swiftly changes the direction of my thoughts.

Here are sample questions:

1. Why is my film a real opportunity for investors?

2. Why am I a good person to be in business with?
3. What good value do I bring to this meeting?
4. Why will they enjoy saying "yes" to my film?

Here are examples of answers that filmmakers provide:

1. Why is my film a real opportunity for investors?
Because we're focusing on a proven demographic that attends movie theaters: African Americans looking for a comedy related to their own experiences.

2. Why am I a good person to be in business with?
Because I'm trustworthy. I meet deadlines. I think through situations. I collaborate well.

3. What good value do I bring to this meeting?
I'm bringing a screenplay that is compelling. The story catches you and doesn't let go.

4. Why will they enjoy saying "yes" to my film?
Because this film has both quality and value in the marketplace . . .
Use the above questions and your own answers to strengthen your resolve. Then you will naturally avoid the appearance of neediness. If you feel any hesitation, do your homework. Improve the elements of your project. Build your confidence on the rock of value. Go forth and share value.

Points to Remember:
• **Darkest Secret:** "Neediness" gives off a smell—and it stinks.
• **Your Countermeasure:**
Empower yourself. Focus on the value you bring to the

studio executive, producer, name actor or private investor. Plan in advance to meet with many people to find the right match. Do your homework with respect to these elements:

1. Focus on the value you bring.

2. You are meeting the other person as a peer.

3. You have the confidence that you're going to meet several people and you're offering the opportunity to do something exciting and profitable.

4. Keep your faith that the right people and right elements will fall into place.

* * *

SECRET #2:
IT'S NOT WHAT YOU CLAIM,
BUT WHAT YOU SHOW THAT COUNTS

Many filmmakers think making a great pitch is about the words—saying the right things. The perfect catch words, the exciting turn of phrase, the tag line that puts the whole thing into focus.

Let's look deeper. First, realize that when speaking, you use your neocortex, the part of your brain devoted to rational thinking.

But when the studio executive listens, she uses her reptile brain to do it.

The neocortex deals with reason, logic, finding patterns. You use it in organizing your DVD collection or filling out a form.

When composing an email message, balancing your checkbook, installing software—the neocortex does what you need. A lot of formal education ends up designed to help train you in using that part of your brain.

But it isn't what you listen with. Our reptile brains don't analyze for the purpose of understanding nor doing an abstract calculation. Rather, that part of the stuff inside our skulls aims for a much more narrow agenda: Survival.

Closely related to the reptile brain is what we call the emotional brain. It too has a single, intense focus: Avoiding loss.

So already, you're in a situation of "disconnect." You're talking from the neocortex and they're listening from the reptile and emotional brains. Never forget a pitch consists of asking someone to take a risk, to put their money down on what cannot help but be a gamble. Odds are, that money will vanish forever. And on some level, they know that. As interested as they may be in taking part in the film making process, as willing as their conscious minds may be to give you a chance, their reptile and emotional brains view everything about you as a threat. Your task is to overcome that. Show them something!

I'll cover three scenarios.

Scenario 1: Pitch to a Name Actor

To pitch to a name actor and get him or her into your film, show a video. Prove that you're a good filmmaker. For example, twin brothers Logan and Noah Miller shot footage of baseball spring training in Tucson, Arizona. Next they used that footage to make a trailer for their feature film *Touching Home*, based on the true story of their relationship with their father. Then, they plotted what they called "the ambush," focusing on meeting Ed Harris, whom they wanted to portray the father.

Harris was to be honored at the San Francisco International Film Festival with a lifetime achievement award. The Miller twin brothers tried a number of different plans, but finally invited a festival team member to ask for two minutes of Harris' time. She agreed. When the time came, the Miller brothers showed Harris their film trailer. In that trailer he noticed Logan throwing well. Harris said, "Nice throw. That was you, wasn't it?"

"Yes, sir," Logan replied.

"See, I can tell you guys apart already . . . I used to be a catcher. Like I told the guy onstage, I always dreamed of playing in the big leagues. Didn't make it as far as you though, only made it to college."

Soon Harris asked, "Do you boys have any actors attached?"

"Brad Dourif."

"Wow . . . You guys must be getting this out there. Brad Dourif is excellent, love his work," Harris said.

After a moment, Harris accepted their screenplay with their business card and a DVD of the trailer. Ultimately, Harris did accept the role and the film was made. Bravo, Miller twins!

Now, how does this all relate to the neocortex/reptile brain dilemma? In showing the trailer, the Miller twins bypassed an actor's reptile brain-concerns with survival. The subconscious thoughts related to the reptile brain might sound like: "Who are these kids? Making a movie with them would torpedo me in the industry."

Further, the trailer quieted the emotional brain, which might sound like: "Working on a tiny, independent film would cost me time and income. Also, this would disrupt my relationship with my agent."

Instead, the trailer excited the pleasure and memory centers of Harris' brain. The trailer created "wanting" in Harris' brain. Enough to accept the screenplay and read it. And that made the Miller twins' pitch successful.

Scenario 2: Pitch to a Potential Investor

If you have a name actor involved with your project, show a video in which he or she addresses the camera.

For example, producer "Susan Ohlee" has convinced a name actor to "attach" himself to her film *She Knows More*. Now Susan needs something better than merely saying to people, "I've got [name actor] attached."

Instead, Susan shows potential investors a video in which the name actor says, "Hi, I'm [name actor] and I'm on board with this film *She Knows More*. This is a great script, and I know that the director Susan Ohlee is really sharp and a good director. So I invite you to invest in this film. I'll see you at the wrap party!"

Do you see how much more power showing a video conveys? So much more personal than merely saying the words, "Oh, yeah. [Name actor] is involved with *She Knows More*."

Some readers will say, "But I don't have a name actor." Then, you lead with whatever impressive element you have. Show a video of a top scientist if your film is about cutting edge science. Show a video of one of your mentors praising your talent and diligent work. Such video testimonials will help you get to the next level. Perhaps at that level, your video testimonials will help you gain a name actor.

And we'll notice that a number of the most successful films had no name actors. Some genres attract higher box office earnings. One film jumps to mind: *Night of the Living Dead*, made for a $114,000 budget and earning $12 million domestically and $18 million internationally.

Scenario 3: Pitch to a Studio Executive

A screenwriter pitches her script and at some point says something like:

"...the tall man slams his fist straight into Mark's jaw. Mark crashes through the window! Nineteen stories up! But —he just manages to grab onto the ledge! There's broken glass everywhere. It cuts into his hands as he holds on for dear life! Blood oozes from the cuts."

The screenwriter is painting a picture in the executive's mind, making him see the action. This is known as creating a *word picture*. You might say, "Good idea." But what helps you the most is understanding why. Your goal is to get the executive to shift mental gears. Remember, he starts by listening with his reptile and emotional brains. No matter what he consciously thinks or believes, his nervous system categorizes you as a possible threat. You must arouse "curiosity and desire," that is, you want him (or her) to emotionally engage with your material. In fact, a top business pitch expert who has successfully raised tens of millions of dollars, Oren Klaff, makes exactly that point. In the end you arouse one of two sets of reactions: either "curiosity and desire" (which puts the listener on your side) or unfortunately you arouse "fear and dislike"—which makes for an unsuccessful pitch.

As we saw in the scenario with Ed Harris, viewing the trailer of the baseball spring training engaged him; his curiosity and desire were stimulated. His love of baseball helped intrigue him with the proposed film.

Writer–director–producer Jerry Zucker (director of the hit movie *Ghost*) once said, "In the movie business, people would much rather watch a 10–minute DVD than read a 120 –page screenplay." So if you have a comedic screenplay, film part of it before an audience and be sure that microphones pick up the laughter from audience members! What does this do? It gets the studio executive to calm fears that the film may not get laughs. You're proving that the material works.

You have other options. You can film short films and place them on YouTube.com. For example, producer – director Sam Raimi (trilogy of *Spider-man* films) hired Uruguayan filmmaker Fede Alvarez as the director of the remake of Raimi's cult hit *The Evil Dead* based on the strength of Alvarez's low–budget YouTube hit short, *Panic Attack!* It's apparent that producer–director Sam Raimi found *Panic Attack!* intriguing; it aroused his curiosity and desire.

Points to Remember:
• **Darkest Secret #1: It's not what you claim, but what you show that counts.**
• **Your Countermeasure:**
Create some kind of film to engage and excite your target audience—an actor, executive, or private investor. Perhaps film a trailer, or a little scene from the script before a live audience, or a testimonial from a name actor interested in the film.

* * * * * *

I first shared the next material in my book, *Darkest Secrets of Film Directing*.

Secret: Some of your best ideas won't work.

George Takei (Lieutenant—later Captain—Sulu of *Star Trek* fame) saved me from a bad scene I had written for a feature film I was directing.

When I met him to discuss a role, he proved gracious. More, the man is funny. His laughter turned out warm and resounding.

I showed some storyboards. One depicted a barely lit scene. One in the morning and our hero sheds a single tear. That single teardrop falls into his tea cup. As it strikes the surface, the teardrop makes a tidal wave in the tea, splashing a tiny tsunami within its porcelain walls. It was like a comet falling into the ocean, but in miniature. All in close up. Extreme close up. Slow motion, too.

At the time, I was so proud of that.

"Uh, Tom?" George asked gently. "Isn't that a bit melodramatic?"

Of course in retrospect I see that scene was a bit melodramatic the same way the North Pole in winter is a bit chilly. I took George's advice and cut the scene. Later, my film gained a distributor, went to the Cannes film market and earned international distribution.

First cuts are a bitch for a director, because it's been so many months and you put your trust in your editor and you're going to see your film assembled for the first time. You look at it and go, This is terrible. I hate it. - Richard Donner (director of Superman *and* Lethal Weapon)

Avoid growling at people who give you feedback. It's like a friend who tells you to remove the spinach on your teeth before you go into a job interview. Or it can be. Depends on who they are. In time you learn to discern whose input makes sense, improves your work. Others won't understand. They'll have nothing worthwhile to offer. Usually. But sometimes a strange idea can spark an improvement. Hence the vital need to encourage feedback and listen to the feedback given (even if you ignore it).

Encourage people to share their opinions. For example, I

say things like:

"I'm glad you brought that up" and "I'm going to really think about that." Even at times when I want to scream defenses for my first ideas. Sometimes my ideas work and sometimes they bear improving.

Steven Spielberg said, "Directing is knowing when to say 'yes.'"

I'll add that directing is also making an atmosphere so people feel comfortable and contribute and you'll be saying 'yes' often. Remain approachable. For example, when actors want to try a take in unusual ways, say, "Let's try it."

Points to Remember:

Secret: Some of your best ideas won't work.

Your Countermeasure:
You don't have to take anyone's advice, but hearing more thoughts gives you more options.

* * * * * *

This next section is material I first shared in my book, *Your Power Path to Freedom, Success and Happiness.*

MOVE AHEAD SUCCESSFULLY
EVEN WHEN YOU'RE CRITICIZED

Do you want real success and fulfillment? Then, learn to handle criticism in an empowered manner. The crucial detail when facing criticism is to prepare to answer your own personal and empowering questions.

1. Does this person really want good things for me?
2. What are my personal goals, and does this comment strengthen me?
3. Does this comment strengthen my work?
4. Does this comment help me learn and grow?

1. Does this person really want good things for me?

I have an extended family member who has nothing but criticism for me. He's older and he's never been an entrepreneur, author, educator or feature film director. Those are my areas of expertise. However, this person just wants to make me "wrong." Wait a minute! This is a family member, but his goal is "to be right" and "to put the other person down." It's sad really.

When you consider whether criticism has merit, consider the source. If someone is in your target market, that criticism may be useful. However, if someone is merely guessing and has never entered the field you're working in, assess whether to dismiss such criticism.

Talking to my negative extended family member would be *where good ideas go to die.* So I often avoid this person. I have a circle of friends and colleagues who are supportive and still provide me with the constructive feedback that may be hard to hear, but their intention is good things for me. I can trust them.

2. What are my personal goals and does this comment strengthen me?

What are your real goals? Do you want to be famous? Do you want to do good artistic work? Do you want to make lots of money? Do you deeply long to express your creativity?

All of the above have different elements attached to them.

It's important for you to be honest with yourself. What do you really want?

The truth is that I want to serve my readers, audiences, graduate students and clients. So I'm willing to hear tough feedback and learn about areas to improve for my projects. For each book I write, I have at least two editors. They can be really tough and they push me to write in better ways. That's what I really want. I do not want to be coddled.

So even if my editors might occasionally clothe a comment with sarcasm, I still know that their comments actually strengthen me. After writing 31 books, I'm a better writer today.

Also, pause and get access to your own intuition. Often, some people are so quick to judge and say, "That won't work." How do they know? And imagine this: If your intuition is correct and you follow your heart—and you succeed—what will they say? They'll merely shrug and mildly reply, "Oh, I guess I was wrong on that one." Do *not* leave your fate to someone else. *Answer your own heart's call.*

To take this conversation to the next step, view my 7 min. video "How to Believe in Yourself When Others Don't" (on YouTube.com).

3. Does this comment strengthen my work?

This is where the real work takes place. A tough comment like "I think that totally fails to engage your target market" may be the best reality check that you need. For example, with a video related to my science fiction franchise *TimePulse*, my team hit a wall. We needed a paragraph to bridge two sections of the video. I had four people tell me that the draft of the paragraph missed the mark. Okay. Back to the drawing board. Eventually, we came up with a solution. With a new approach, we found an appropriate quote to bridge the sections. [See our 1 minute video of science fiction and action, *TimePulse,* on YouTube.com—Search for "TimePulse Tom Marcoux."]

4. Does this comment help me learn and grow?

My team members know that I can calmly listen to any comment that points out flaws in a draft of a project. I'll often ask follow-up questions. Why? I'm focused on learning and growing as an artist in the various fields I participate in: speaking, writing, filmmaking and art direction of graphic novels.

My point is that a truly creative person must develop a "thick skin" and also run criticism through a filter. Some critical comments have nothing to do with your goals. Let them flow past like leaves on a stream of water.

Other comments, given as support and which strengthen your work, may raise your work to world-class level. It's an adventure that is actually worth the pain and effort. It's a road that includes surprising, happy moments.

Consider writing your own answers in a personal journal to these questions:

What are your real goals with your project/career? Who has the real feedback that can help you improve your project? Reflect deeply: Who do you want to support your work but the person simply does *not* support your work? Where else can you look for real support and guidance (a coach*, an instructor, someone else)?

* After working with my own coaches/mentors, I continue as an Executive Coach – Spoken Word Strategist, helping my clients Move Forward Faster. My phrase is: *Take Command, Focus Your Brand.*

* * * * * *

I first shared this material at my blog YourBodySoulandProsperity.com.

Don't Let Your Fear Shut Down Your Dream! —Move Forward

Fear can strangle your dream. Just as bad, fear can paralyze you. Many people get stuck because they cannot do something perfectly. That is, their fear of appearing "imperfect" stops them from taking action. Perfection has its place—like when a surgeon operated on one of my family members years ago. However, most things only need excellence. So... *set your own criteria for excellence.* That is, identify what you must do to make the project excellent. Let go of perfect. Focus on excellence. How? Ask yourself these questions before you take action on a new project:

1. What must be in this project?
2. What can be left out?
3. How long do you have to work on it?
4. What does the end user expect to find in this project?
5. How can you surprise and delight the end user?

These questions and your answers serve as a starting point for a strategic plan. When you develop such a plan, you can *set criteria for excellence.*

You decide what is most important for your project.

As an Executive Coach, I help my client set up a strategic plan. Even better, we identify how my client can take important steps forward even while feeling fear.

From interviewing a number of successful people, one theme arises: The successful person took effective action even while feeling fear.

Don't let your fear shut down your dream! That is, do not let your energy be wasted in trying to gain approval from everyone. The fear of loss of approval can paralyze many of us.

Instead of focusing on approval, focus on truly living your life in a joyful and fulfilling way. Your joyful life is built on listening to your heart and intuition.

Your intuition calls you to expand, to experiment, and to take an appropriate risk.

Your fear calls you to contract, to hide, to avoid an appropriate risk.

Heed the call of your heart and your intuition.

I have faced fear many times: acting in feature films, directing my first feature film, speaking to large audiences, singing in a band, recording my first audio book, appearing as a guest expert on television, and other occasions. The idea is to avoid waiting for fear to go away. Instead, seek to quiet fear down a bit.

To quiet down your fear, set your criteria for excellence. Consciously focus on letting go of trying "to be perfect" and "to get everyone to like you" or "to get everyone to like your project."

"The only things I regret... are the things I didn't do."
– Joe Karbo

"Go to the effort. Invest the time. Write the letter. Make the apology. Take the trip. Purchase the gift. Do it. The seized opportunity renders joy. The neglected brings regret."
– *Max L. Lucado*

Take a step forward.

I know this to be true. In directing my first feature film, I filmed the first scene until I filmed the last scene. I edited the first sequence until I edited the last sequence. It was all one step after another.

"You don't learn to walk by following rules. You learn by doing, and by falling over." – *Richard Branson*

Do something today toward realizing your dream.

May you enjoy your journey and expressing creativity.

Tom

Tom Marcoux
Creator/Art Director of *Jack AngelSword* trilogy of graphic novels
Speaker-Author of 31 books—free chapters on Amazon.com
Executive Coach – Spoken Word Strategist
CEO leading teams in the United Kingdom, India and USA

ABOUT THE AUTHOR

Tom Marcoux won a special award at the **Emmys.** Tom wrote, directed, and produced a feature film that went to **Cannes film market**, where it gained international distribution. Tom has performed as leading actor in two feature films and had roles in commercials and other projects. He is engaged in the book/film projects *Jack AngelSword* (fantasy-thriller) and *Jenalee Storm.*

His graphic novel *Crystal Pegasus* is available on Amazon.com. View free chapters of his previous fiction collection *TimePulse: Beyond Titanic* at Amazon.com.

Tom Marcoux is the author of three film/TV industry related books:

- *Darkest Secrets of the Film and Television Industry Every Actor Should Know:* A Film Director and Actor Reveals Methods for Your Acting, Auditions, Movie Roles and Self-Promotion.
- *Darkest Secrets of Film Directing:* How Successful Film Directors Overcome Hidden Traps
- *Darkest Secrets of Making a Pitch for Film and Television:* How You Can Get a Studio Executive, Producer, Name Actor or Private Investor to Say "Yes" to Your Project

Tom helps people like you **fulfill big dreams.** Known as an Executive Coach – Spoken Word Strategist and TFG Thought Leader, Tom has authored 31 books with sales in 15 countries. One of his *Darkest Secrets* books rose to #1 on Amazon.com Hot New Releases in Business Life (and in Business Communication). He guides clients and audiences (IBM, Sun Microsystems, etc.) to success in leadership, team building, job interviewing, public speaking, media relations, and branding. A member of the National Speakers

Association, he is a professional coach and guest expert on TV, radio, and print, and was dubbed "the Personal Branding Instructor" by the *San Francisco Examiner.*

Tom addressed the National Association of Broadcasters' Conference six years running. With a degree in psychology, Tom is a guest lecturer at **Stanford University**, DeAnza, and California State University, and he teaches public speaking, science fiction cinema/literature and comparative religion at Academy of Art University.

See Tom's popular blogs:

TomSuperCoach.com

BeHeardandBeTrusted.com

YourBodySoulandProsperity.com

Tom Marcoux can help you with **speech writing** and **coaching for your best performance.**

As Tom says, *Make Your Speech a Pleasant Beach.*

Join Tom's Linkedin.com group: *Executive Public Speaking and Communication Power.*

At Google+: join the community "Create Your Best Life – Charisma & Confidence"

Get a **Free** report: "9 Deadly Mistakes to Avoid for Your Next Speech and 9 Surefire Methods" at

http://tomsupercoach.com/freereport9Mistakes4Speech.html

Tom Marcoux has trained CEOs, small business owners, and graduate students to speak with impact and gain audiences' tremendous approval and cooperation. *Learn how to present and get thunderous applause!*

"Tom Marcoux coached me to get more done in 10 days than other coaches in 2 years." Brad Carlson, CEO of Mindstrong LLC

"Tom, Thanks for your coaching and work with me on revising my speech at a major university. Working with you has been so enlightening for me. Through your gentle prodding and guidance I was able to write a speech that connects with the audience. I wish everyone could experience the transformation I have undergone. You have helped me discover the warm and compelling stories that now make my speech reach hearts and uplift minds. This was truly an empowering experience. I cannot thank you enough for your great assistance." — J.S.

"Tom Marcoux has been an NAB Conference favorite [speaker] for six years. And he is very energetic."
– John Marino,
Vice President, National Association of Broadcasters,
Washington, D.C.

"Using just one of Tom Marcoux's methods, I got more done in 2 weeks than in 6 months."
– Jaclyn Freitas, M.A.

Become a fan of Tom's graphic novels/feature films:
Fantasy Thriller: *Jack AngelSword*
type "JackAngelSword" at Facebook.com

Science fiction: *TimePulse*
www.facebook.com/timepulsegraphicnovel

Children's Fantasy: *Crystal Pegasus*
www.facebook.com/crystalpegasusandrose
See **Free Chapters** of Tom Marcoux's 31 books
at http://amzn.to/ZiCTRj

Special Offer Just for Readers of this Book:

Contact Tom Marcoux at tomsupercoach@gmail.com for special discounts on books, coaching, workshops and presentations. Just mention your experience with this book.

www.ingramcontent.com/pod-product-compliance
Lightning Source LLC
Chambersburg PA
CBHW070555180626
46817CB00005B/1855